The Taking of Stonecrop

The Taking of Stonecrop

E.D.E. Bell

Atthis Arts, LLC

THE TAKING OF STONECROP

Cover illustration by Anna Rettberg
Map of Fayen by G.C. Bell
Editorial Services by Herta B. Feely, Chrysalis Editorial
Story Consulting by G.C. Bell, M. Cusack, and B. McKee

Published by Atthis Arts, LLC
Centerville, Ohio
www.atthisarts.com

First Edition: Published February 2014

ISBN: 978-0-9896992-4-2

17 16 15 14   1 2 3 4 5 6 7 8 9 10

This story is dedicated to Nancy Ebert,

who taught me to be brave.

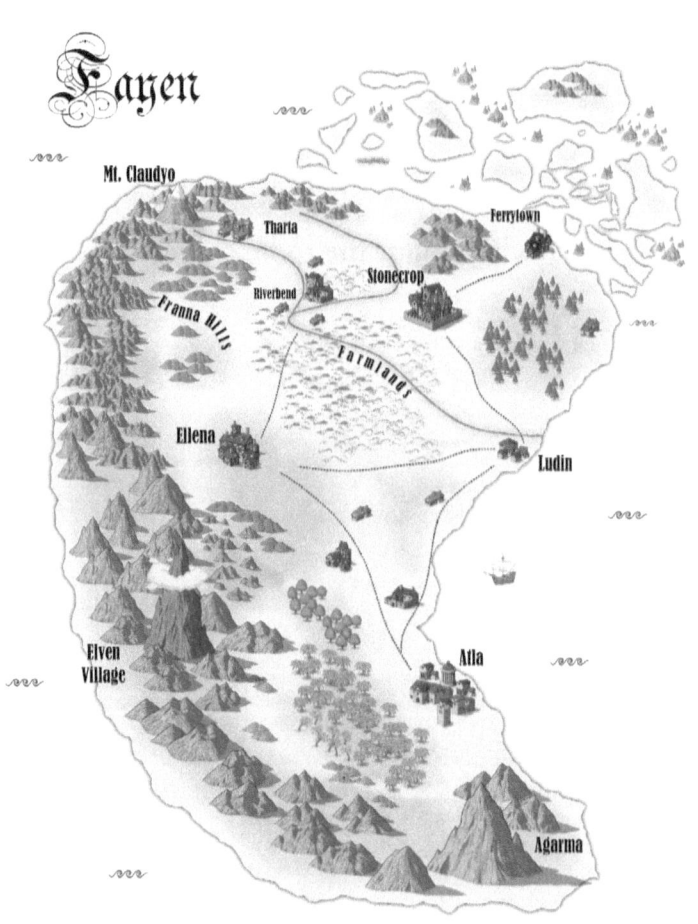

The Taking of Stonecrop

Part I – The Royal River

As his children stood watch beside his bed, the King drew his final breath.

Silence filled the lofty room, and the Steward gestured reverently over his chest.

"It is done," Fisk stated, looking up at the Steward expectantly. "I thank you for your service, but your duties are no longer required."

The Steward's eyes flashed but he made no immediate move to leave. He bowed slightly, perhaps too slightly. "Your Highness." Only then did the Steward step slowly across the room. He hesitated just a moment as he reached the doorway, but then he continued on and was soon out of sight.

This left Fisk, his sister Byrn, and the corpse of their father spread between them. Fisk spoke quickly and with a hint of anticipation to his voice. "I do not wish to make this unpleasant," Fisk said, his eyes narrowing, "but your continued presence in the castle would be . . . confusing. Be on your way by dark, and be seen by no one."

Byrn's cheeks flushed in shock. She had known in that final exhale that Fisk was now King, but to order her out of her own home? Her mind spun, and she heard the words come from her mouth almost as if someone else were speaking them.

"You have no right to—" Byrn stopped as Fisk reached for the hilt of his sword. The situation began to clarify in her mind, and she looked up in disgust.

"The peasants will be told that in your grief, you flung yourself from the King's tower. They will mourn your tragic loss either way. It is your choice whether they mourn over an actual body or just the idea of one." Fisk tossed his long, wavy hair, a habit he had picked up during his years of being praised and catered to, for no reason other than people's understanding that someday he would rule them. He was tall, handsome, and his golden eyes shone in the lamplight.

Byrn's eyes fixed on her brother's slightly turned smile. It was as though she was seeing him—truly seeing him—for the first time. Despite his regal mane and flawless features, his excited grin was repulsive. *When did this happen?* Byrn wondered to herself. *Why didn't I see it?* "You're a monster," she whispered.

Fisk laughed. "Cute, Toady. Just like old times."

Byrn winced. Did Fisk think this was a game? That he was challenging her to skip stones across the fountains, rather than threatening her life? He continued as if he hadn't noticed. "You know as well as I do that our father was weak, tired. If you had traveled as I have, you would see that the kingdom has long been slipping from his grasp. The subjects are insolent, whining about petty grievances—not showing proper deference to their liege, and begrudging small requests of tribute. Our nation needs a strong king, not a sickly old man or his . . . homely princess."

Fisk stared at Byrn pointedly, then took a step toward her. "We are no longer playmates, and I have great matters to which I must attend. Gather your personal things, and take whatever coin you need to be comfortable, but do it quickly. I took an oath to protect you, and I consider this act of mercy to be the fulfillment of that oath. But if I ever see your face again, you will die."

Byrn held herself steady; she would not let Fisk see her cry. And Fisk was the Elder; the throne was his. He had prepared for this betrayal while she had not even considered the possibility.

But over the years while she had tended to her father during his lengthy illness, the King as well as the Steward had taught her a great deal about strategy—more than Fisk realized. She knew that right now what was essential was to survive. Still without a full understanding of why Fisk would do such a thing, her father's training snapped into her mind. He had always emphasized that timing was key. *Sense the moment,* he had told her. *And when you get that feeling—of right or wrong, you must be prepared to change plans in that instant.* And she had that feeling now.

Whatever Fisk was up to, he held the better terrain, the strategic advantage. It *felt* wrong and she knew instinctively that retreat was her best move, to avoid risking further harm. She bowed slowly, allowing the chestnut curls in her hair to brush the boards beneath her. "My liege."

She slipped out of the room, noting that the halls had been cleared of the host of people who would normally walk them. She rushed to her quarters passing no attendants, hearing none of the usual banter of the servants. She felt as though time itself had stopped to wait for her to leave. Once inside her bedroom, Byrn threw no glances at the royal dresses or her collection of gems. They were only a liability.

She hastily threw items into a laundry bag that she had pulled from the servants' closet. Essential items only: a flask, some cloth, a small dish, and a mending kit she had no idea how to use. A couple of small knives followed, along with enough gold coins to buy whatever else she needed once somewhere safe. She searched the small shelves next to the fireplace, and was pleased to find a flint and a small bottle of oil.

She closed her eyes. She would need something more, but something Fisk would never miss. *Of course.* She rummaged in the drawers of her wardrobe, glancing around cautiously before slipping the item into the sack.

Byrn held her breath, cursing, as she squeezed into a simple dress. *Next time, I will select more portly servants.* She grinned at her absurd dilemma, despite the circumstance. It was a trait she shared with her father, who had believed in humor as a remedy for all things. Fisk would not know this, of course. He had never been a child, always a prince. And he had believed humor was a weakness, a vulnerability to be exploited. Being the older child, he had been obsessed with the throne, paying very little attention to anything not related to that objective.

Byrn did not know whether this mirthless demeanor had been Fisk's choice, or forced upon him by the administrators of the fortress. But either way, all those hours spent with the Blademaster, the Commanding General, and the Chancellor had hardened him. *Everyone needs to laugh, even you, brother.* Byrn's smile faded, again recalling that now, as she packed, crowds were likely gathering to mourn both her father's long-expected death as well as her own untimely one. She shook her head. *There is no time for this.*

Fortunately, a pair of thick-soled boots fit better than the overburdened dress, and Byrn wrapped herself in a felted cloak and headed for a back entrance. She thought briefly of visiting the stables, but even disguised they might know her voice, for as much time as she spent there. No, she could not risk being recognized by anyone until she had time to think things through. Her face hidden, she slipped out past the guards, who only saw the standard cloak of a castle servant and whistled slightly before muttering something Byrn chose to ignore.

As the banks of the Royal River came into view, Byrn stopped suddenly, digging the metal toes of her boots into the mud. A torrent of thoughts ran through her mind as she tried to understand why she was here like this at all. Just this morning, her father, even in his fevered stupor, had whispered that he loved her. How was she now running from her own home, wearing her servant's dress, and without even a horse to speed her journey? What threat could she possibly pose to Fisk's rule? The throne was his. He was young, strong, and powerful. Why would he exile her, threaten her? It made no sense.

Tears ran down her face, but Byrn did not pay them mind as they rolled off of her cheeks, falling into the mud below. The pain of losing her father fresh in her chest like a critical wound, she could not even begin to understand Fisk's aims, or how she should proceed.

She considered leaving it all behind. She had plenty of gold, more in her humble laundry sack than most common folk would see in a lifetime. She could marry, raise children, and start a life that would truly be her own. Nobody would suspect who she really was, and she could die peacefully of old age, surrounded by a loving family. It was a compelling vision, and it pulled at her forcefully, like the river's current itself.

She lifted a foot, then set it down again. Her stomach felt tight, sick, and she could not bring herself to move forward. That knot within her ached, the one her father had always called the, "inner guide." Her father had made her promise that she would trust it. And though she didn't want to listen, she knew with certainty what it was telling her.

Fisk could not be allowed to rule. If a man could threaten to kill his own sister, to betray her over the still-warm body of their own father, then he could not be trusted with the well-being of her father's people, of *her* people. They were her people, after all. Her father had ingrained in her that responsibility.

The knot inside of her loosened, just slightly. Yet she hated the feel of it. Court politics had always been a necessary evil, one with which she had coexisted simply because she knew that Fisk would eventually rule, not herself. She picked up a small stone and heaved it fiercely into the river below. Then she swore under her breath, the sort of unnecessarily vulgar thing that served no purpose other than to horrify proper folk. But, she admitted to herself, it made her feel momentarily better. She glanced around, wondering if any forest animals had heard her. For good measure, she uttered it again then turned her gaze back down at the water below.

So, then, was she meant to oppose him? Depose him and take the throne herself? Usurping well-established tradition was unconscionable, but no more so than what Fisk himself had done. The image of Fisk, smirking gleefully at her as she fled his presence was burned into her eyes. She closed them, but it did not go away. She was disoriented, stunned. She understood that she needed time—time to gather information, time to plan. Time to better understand Fisk's motives. She could not stay here, but she could move on, and survive.

Some plans could wait, but one decision could not. She knew that this first decision was critical, as the choice of battlefield was often crucial. She needed a large city to blend in and begin to gather support. A village or town would not suffice. Of the three major cities in Fayen, Atla was too far away – though her cousins would welcome her there, she couldn't allow Fisk enough time to establish himself, in ways positive or negative. Change was more difficult to accept once people had become accustomed to something. And Fisk could not be given time to marry and produce an heir.

A chill began to set through her limbs and she knew it was time to decide. Should she head south, through the farmlands, to Ellena? Or head east, along the river, to Stonecrop? The river rushed in patterns before her, as if urging her to choose.

The choice was not obvious. Ellena was the larger city of the two, bustling and thriving on a wide range of trade and craft, but its people might be more difficult to sway. The people of Ellena were industrious and freethinking. Knowing the extent to which the crown relied on their goods and revenue, the people, led by the Merchants' Guild, had established a tenuous truce with the monarchs over the years. Yet even toward the nobles they felt no devotion, only a sense of grudging acceptance.

Stonecrop was a more traditional culture, at least as her family had perceived it. The Church had established its base there, and though they were practical enough not to admit it to the monarchs, the people saw the Holy Father in the Cathedral as a greater authority than the King, locked away in his fortress, or the local Duke, who also deferred most of the rule to the

Church. The people of Stonecrop were hardworking and faithful, more predisposed to ceremony and tradition.

Both held advantages. The people of Stonecrop would be more reverent toward her bloodline, easier to engage in matters of politics and power. They would have a greater yearning for a stable throne, if she could convince them that Fisk was not suitable. Yet the people of Ellena were more creative, with great wealth and ability to assist, and they already held no love for her brother. She paused, looking up into the trees. *A revolutionary would choose Ellena. The future Queen would choose Stonecrop.*

And so, a servant's cloak on her back and a laundry bag tied around her chest, the recently deceased Princess Byrn of Riverbend Fortress trudged east toward Stonecrop.

Byrn had traveled to Stonecrop many times with her father. With access to swift vessels and carriages, the journey took only days. On foot and not conditioned to finding her own food and water, it took her at least the course of a full mooncycle. She wasn't precisely sure, having lost count of the days.

She was not prepared for the hardships of traveling alone. It was more difficult to find food along the riverbank than her teachers had led her to believe, and her stomach pinched and ached. The gold she carried grew heavy in her sack, and more than once she considered leaving it behind. The ground was rocky, and she tripped over hidden tree roots while dodging the immense spider webs that otherwise dragged across her face. The scratches on her hands never seemed to heal, and there were days on end when it rained, and she yearned for the simple feeling of being dry again.

But there was nothing for it but to grit her teeth and push forward. The brisk air stung her lungs as she marched, and she distracted herself by concentrating on planning for the days ahead. Once she arrived, she knew she had plenty of money for an inn or even to buy her own place, but a woman living alone in the city would draw attention that she didn't want. Not yet.

The bridge came into view just as the tall spire of the Stonecrop Cathedral appeared beneath the clouds ahead. Her legs burned, and her stomach ached. She wanted only to find the first inn that she could, throw a gold piece onto the bar, and collapse into the largest, most comfortable bed that they owned. But this was not her plan, and she knew she needed to be deliberate.

It grew dark as the dirt road slowly turned to cobbled streets, the shopkeepers barely sparing her a glance as she passed. She envisioned the districts of Stonecrop in her mind, for she knew she needed to walk with confidence, blending in as best she could. Despite its devout culture, Stonecrop was not a safe place for a woman to be walking alone.

She gazed longingly ahead at the center of town—the towering Cathedral spire on one side, and the long outer walls of the Duke's estate on the other. She shook her head. Her brother would keep an eye out for her in these places, especially at first, and the risk of being betrayed was high. She did wish she could visit the Duke, a friendly man who had always had a warm smile for her when she had been in the city.

The Duke of Stonecrop was her father's cousin, far enough down the line of succession to pose no real threat, especially with her own cousins off providing a loose rule over Atla and the people of the southern lands. It was a clever arrangement, the people of Atla being more interested in art than politics, and her aunt and cousins perfectly happy to stay there, able to effectively rule without threatening her father's—and now her brother's—hold over the more populous lands of the North.

The Duke had once given her a tiny stuffed bear, with cheerful little glass eyes that twinkled as if it knew something that you didn't. It was a small gesture, but after Fisk had ridiculed it for being a baby's toy, she had hidden the bear, only taking it out when she was alone in her quarters. Her hand slipped into the laundry bag, checking subconsciously that the bear was safe.

No, despite the temptation to barge in on the Duke and cry into the kind man's arms, she could not yet trust anyone of royal lineage, not without better information. *Information,* she reminded herself. *Concentrate, Byrn.*

She took a hard turn, walking away from the center of town, and to an area simply called "The Crescent." It was an area of craftsmen and traders that had formed around the edges of the originally settled area. She looked for the right kind of inn, one that would serve as a gathering place and attract the right sort of people. After passing several inns by, she saw a wooden sign swinging in the evening breeze, adorned with an image of an owl. The owl was reading a book, while wearing a perplexed expression. She couldn't help but chuckle. *What an absurd idea!*

She took a deep breath, looking down at her servant's dress, which now fit perfectly after her long journey. Smiling, she pushed in through the door. A woman swept in front of her. "Good evening, Miss. Welcome to the Brown Owl. Of what help may I be?"

Byrn looked nervously at the woman before her. The innkeeper was tall, with wispy light blonde hair, touched with gray around the edges. She wore a light blue dress, decorated only with a touch of old lace at the collar and sleeves. Over the top she wore a stained linen apron into which a tiny flower had been embroidered. Over one of her arms she carried an oversized basket filled with used utensils and food scraps. The basket swung slightly.

In return, the innkeeper appraised the young woman at her door. Byrn's curly hair was pulled behind her head into a knot, and her cream-colored skin was marked with several tiny scars. Her eyes, a brilliant blue, would have been pretty had they not seemed slightly small for her round face, instead giving her a perpetual look of confusion. She looked to be a nice enough girl, and so the innkeeper waited patiently for a response.

Byrn lowered her eyes, curtsying far too excessively for a place like this. Any good servant would have responded more appropriately, but then again she wasn't a good servant.

"Good evening, Lady. I have traveled on foot from Ludin, after my mother's death. I was hoping for a . . . change of scenery to clear my mind. But I have no family here, so I am looking for temporary work until I can settle in." Byrn bowed her head submissively.

The innkeeper snorted loudly. "You'd have to get up pretty early to bake your biscuits with my shortening, girl." She shook her head, looking over humorously over at the man who had emerged from the kitchen. "It's a fair story, but you don't have a touch of the sound of Ludin, and your robes are standard castle issue. I'm half a mind to send you right back out that door."

The woman hesitated. Byrn curtsied, trying to remember how her servants would have answered. "I'm sorry, Lady, it wasn't that I meant any deceiving, it's that I got into a bit of trouble. Best to be forgotten, surely, but, well." Byrn cast her eyes downward. "It's that I'm not allowed to return to the castle. And I've nowhere to go."

The innkeeper rubbed her wrists as she gazed at Byrn for a long moment. "Well," she said, "with a brain like that, you'd be working the square within the day, and I hate to see that of a young girl. And I could use some help. Now, does your trouble involve nosegrain, trouble with the Church, or—she glanced down at Byrn's belly—a family situation?"

Byrn looked away, adopting her best impersonation of shame. A month ago, she might not have known how, but the days picking her way through the forest had humbled her substantially. It was not much of a stretch to look tired and embarrassed. "I'm sorry for lying, Lady. The mistress of service, she said I, well, it's not something I want to discuss. But the trouble, it wasn't those things you said. Nothing like that."

Byrn turned to the side, as if unable to meet the woman's eyes. "Name's Edra. And I'll work so hard, Lady," she muttered.

"Name's Dot. If you pull your weight, I'll give you a room downstairs. If I don't like you for any reason, you're out immediately."

Byrn nodded obediently.

Byrn set up a tiny apartment in the cellar. She burned the clothes from the castle and replaced them with a plain brown dress, one that drew little attention. She bought a heavy chest with a secure lock for the items she had taken from the castle, and wore the key on a chain around her neck, hidden from view; the chest she kept under her bed. She knew that the locked chest would have been suspicious if anyone had seen it, but she was cognizant that she still held enough gold within it to buy and sell Dot's inn a hundred times over without even blinking.

Over the next couple of weeks, Byrn learned the basics of working at an inn. Dot's conviction that Edra was a bit slow helped cover for the simple things Byrn didn't immediately know how to do, as did's Byrn's humility and kindness. In that short period of time, Dot grew very fond of the girl and, thankfully, didn't ask any more questions about her departure from the castle staff.

She listened intently to the news from the travelers and merchants passing through. Usually the talk revolved around the dealings of the local traders, though occasionally the disparaging of a stubborn wife or ungrateful son dominated the evening's banter.

Sometimes the patrons whispered rumors about secret affairs between the townsfolk, though Byrn was skeptical how often the stories could be real. If it happened as often as they claimed, there would be no marriages in the city left to betray. In fact, she had counted six stories about the chandler's wife alone. Byrn often wished to meet the woman, to see what allure she truly held. Again, if she were to believe any of it at all.

Each night Byrn retired to her nook, recording the descriptions of the patrons, particularly those repeat visitors to the inn itself, or those who frequently enjoyed an evening of warm food and lively tales before returning to their homes. She left out the exploits of the chandler's wife, having gained somewhat of a sympathetic affection for the woman.

One evening, as Byrn balanced two pitchers of warm spiced wine on a tray, a trader began talking about the new policies of the King. Byrn's ears perked up.

"He's a tyrant," the man growled, setting his goblet onto the warped old table with a thump, as the other men at the table shifted uncomfortably. "He lives in a castle, but he thinks it's too small of a castle. Already building plans for a larger one, they say. Only thing, he needs more gold to do it properly. Bet he dreams of crapping in a gold pot, that one."

The trader laughed at his own joke before continuing. "Already, we've been told our tribute must increase. All goods are to be inspected. One tariff to leave a city. Another to enter. Another to sell the goods. The boy will be the death of our businesses unless we confront him first."

As Byrn set down the pitchers, another man sitting at the trader's table glanced around nervously. "The walls listen in such places, friend. I would keep these thoughts to yourself, and clarify that your wine has caused you to jest."

The man slid his goblet around between his hands, the wine sloshing recklessly back and forth. "I don't give a dog's balls anymore who hears what. The boy is a brute, and everyone who ever dealt personally with his father knows it. The King himself would have tossed him into the river had he not cared so deeply for the boy's mother. We were fools to have waited until the old man died. Intervention was due long before now, and everyone knows it."

Byrn tensed. Who was this man, talking about her family as though they were normal people? She nosed forward, toward the man's table. He was not hard to hear, as through the course of his rant he had picked up his volume.

"The Guild, they are fighting back, you know. And if you don't want to see our families fall into ruin, you'd be best to support them. If it comes to war, you'll want to be on the right side of it."

At the mention of war, Byrn turned sharply, nearly spilling the wine. Her eyes met those of a man at the counter, who had spun around almost as sharply as she had. The man had seemed a harmless local drunk. Why would political talk interest him so? The man glanced back at her, and Byrn blushed. It made no sense for a barmaid to show such interest either. She would need to be more careful.

"But, he is the King," a man at the table stammered, staring down at the table.

The trader snorted. "A man is only King with the support of his people. Without us, he is nothing."

"Surely, you don't mean that?" a man gasped from another table. "Our King!"

"Surely, I do. What do they provide, the royalty? They sit around in the castle that we built them with our own sweat and cleverness. They take our coin, cut it in half, then give it back to our own neighbors in their benevolence."

Byrn's face grew warm. Her brother was a brute, there she agreed. But the royalty, they provided much to the common people: security, food for the poor, cultivation of the arts. These people, how could they understand? She turned away quickly to hide her flushed face, both from the trader's table and particularly from the man listening intently at the bar.

Stopped by the sound of a throat clearing behind her, Byrn turned to face Dot, who was glaring at her with a root peeler in hand. Byrn rushed back into the kitchen to help prepare a fresh barrel of potatoes, nodding her head obediently as Dot gave her a few choice words about what happens to girls who eavesdrop on the customers.

When she finally emerged, her fingers were sore from the small peeler, and the angry trader had left. In addition, the bar was empty where the suspiciously interested drunk had been seated.

She burned an extra candle that night, recording the details of the evening's events.

The man at the bar did not return the next night, nor the night after. This irritated Byrn, as it only proved that he was not who he claimed to be. A man simply wishing for a cup of forgetting would not be scared away by political discussion.

But the other man, the angry one, returned again a few days later. Sober this time—at least at first—he spoke in whispers to a group of half a dozen men who had gathered around the table in the corner.

Byrn bustled about that evening, not giving Dot any reason to be cross with her, and so she only caught snippets of the conversation. She scrubbed an empty stew pot over the sink, while piecing together what she had heard. Dot rested an arm on her dress. "You're a fine worker, Edra. If you ever wish to talk to me about what you've done, I may be able to help. Things are never so bad as they seem."

Flooded with gratitude, Byrn smiled at the woman who had treated her with such mercy. She nodded slightly. "Your kindness shall not be forgotten."

Dot laughed, chuckling. "Now don't go taking on airs, young lady. I admit I've gotten used to you washing the pots for me. Finally able to use my hands again, you know." She rubbed her hands together. "Not so stiff when I'm able to rest them."

Byrn silently scolded herself for letting her guard down. She gave the woman a quick hug, and returned to scouring a particularly stubborn spot.

When the man left that evening, Byrn slipped out behind him. "Sir?"

"Don't want any, girl. Got other things on my mind."

Byrn was glad the darkness concealed her blush at the man's assumption. "No, Sir, it's about . . . the King."

She could not see his reaction, but his sudden silence caused her to rush her words. "I come from the castle, from Riverbend Fortress. It is a secret, but I used to work there. I heard you mention war the other night. And tonight, you, well, I heard some of it tonight again. Could you explain? Just . . . to ease my mind?"

The man hesitated, before grunting. "I'm not used to worrying women over such things. Seems you folk have enough to do without fretting over the affairs of men."

It was best that he could not see Byrn's eyes roll as she formulated a response. "Yes, well, I understand, of course. But, you see, I'm already worrying. I have friends—old friends—at the Riverbend Fortress. It is only for their safety that I ask you. I—" Byrn forced herself to sniffle, "I would not be able to sleep after what I heard tonight. Not if . . . there is a war coming."

"Well, I suppose it's nothing you won't hear on the streets anyway." The man cleared his throat. "The Merchants' Guild has started an uprising against the King. It was brewing for years, and the swift actions of his new royal asshole have ignited it like an overfilled powder keg. The Guild is gathering a force in the fields outside of Ellena, and the King has pledged to see every one of them dead. But the Guild has deep enough pockets; they will see to it that they gather two men for every one of the King's. Royal Army won't stand a chance, if it comes to it."

Byrn knew she should be more cautious, but she needed to know more. "The Guild has started an uprising? The Merchants' Guild of Ellena? What has the new King done to anger them so?" Byrn glanced around her. Her eyes were adjusting to the dark, and she began to see the silhouette of the man, cast by a tiny gleam of moonlight.

"Oh, nothing really," the man answered, a sneer in his voice. "Greater demands of tribute. New regulations on trade.

A few beheadings to show he is serious about it all. Not to mention murdering the Princess." Byrn gasped, quickly covering her mouth. "Well, he didn't expect us to buy that absurd story, did he? Leapt from the tower in her grief? Who wrote that, one of his pages? Smart move, though. The Duke is old, and relatively unknown in Ellena. The others in line are far away, on the other side of Fayen. The people have nobody to rally behind. Ripe for the Guild to step in."

Byrn saw the shadow of the man moving away. "Look, I'm sorry, girl. Nobody likes war. But the way things are going, the blood of the Royal Army is going to flow, and it's best to be on the right side of it. That's why I'm here, anyway."

She could hear his footsteps moving even farther away. He was nearly gone. "You're recruiting an army," she called out, in a piercing whisper. "To oppose the King." The man did not respond. "There is something I must tell you. Something you must know." The man's footsteps stopped, and she could sense him turning slowly back, toward her.

But just then, a large hand wrapped itself around her mouth, and she felt herself being dragged off.

Part II: The Secret of Stonecrop

Byrn kicked and tried to scream, until she realized she was no match for the strong arms that were lifting her into a cart. She calmed herself, recognizing that her captors were being careful with her, given the circumstance. Knowing there was nothing she could do at the moment anyway, she relaxed and tried to listen. But there was no conversation, and very little sound. The wheels of the cart were well oiled, the horses calm. Only the sound of the horses' hooves, and the wooden wheels turning against the smooth stones of the streets broke the tense silence.

After a bit, her mouth was uncovered. A voice whispered in her ear, "If you call out, you will be silenced in a less pleasant way. If you remain quiet, you will be treated fairly."

The cart continued to roll along, but Byrn estimated they were still somewhere in town. Eventually the cart stopped, and her captors remained perfectly silent, though she could hear the deep creak of a large door opening. Then they started up again and she felt the cart moving downward, and soon she could see only the dancing shadows of candlelight on what appeared to be the walls of some sort of underground passageway. The cart halted again, and a hand reached for hers. It was a plain hand, with several old scars, and no jewelry. She reached for it, and stepped out of the cart.

She found herself face to face with a man who was barely her own height. His hair was cropped short, and his manner of dress was common. There was nothing much to note about him except perhaps the keenness of his gaze, which was fixed directly upon her. "Your Highness. I apologize for the way you were treated, but we could not risk you giving away your secret to a mere mercenary, paid by the Merchants' Guild to stir people to war."

Your Highness. She would have time for that question later, but for now she had no indication anyone meant her harm. She looked around and saw she was at the entrance to a large room. If it could be called a room—it was rounded as though carved into the underground stone. Long tables filled the room, which was lit by an abundance of brightly burning torches. Several men and women, who appeared as though they had been busy at work prior to her arrival, stopped and bowed before her.

"Bowing to a dead princess," she muttered under her breath. In the clear voice she had been trained to use before a crowd, she stated, "I will learn of you, and you of me. But until we have had a chance to know each other better, you will not bow, and you will call me by the name Edra."

Several of the people nodded appreciatively, returning to going about their business as if nothing of note had just happened. The man at her side waved a hand, and the cart pulled back down the tunnel. He turned back to Byrn. "Klev," the man said. "Klev Dwarve. I am the leader of this organization, which consists of my family. I was a friend of your father's; he was a good man. I was sorry to hear of his passing."

Byrn looked at him skeptically. "He never mentioned you."

"Good." Klev grimaced. "That was our arrangement. There are things going on in this world—things you do not understand, but soon will." He paused, and Byrn put on a stern expression.

"There was no need to escort me in such a manner. I had not entirely decided whether to reveal myself to that man or not. I was gathering information. If he was part of a group opposing the King, perhaps I could have—"

She stopped, realizing that Klev stood politely, waiting for her to finish, but that the man had no interest in what she was saying. Byrn gave up on her tale, closing her mouth awkwardly.

"Perhaps we misunderstood your intentions." He smiled. "But no matter, you're here now."

Byrn was confused, and felt irritated by the cryptic introduction. "Who are you exactly?"

"As I said, we are the Dwarves." Klev smiled, his eyes glinting in the torchlight. "Do you believe in magic, Byrn?"

Ignoring the man's unauthorized use of her real name, she answered carefully. "One's beliefs are very personal; I'm sure you agree."

"I do, actually. But it doesn't matter whether you believe in them or not. They're real, as sure as you or I stand here."

"What's real?" Byrn started to grow frustrated.

Klev saw her expression change, and decided he'd better get to it. "My family works for a race of magical creatures who claim the Creator Himself made them so that they could protect people, as well as other animals. These protectors look much as we do, though if you are around them enough you come to see the difference. They are larger than most people, and the men and women look about the same."

Byrn tried to keep her response calm. "Magic people, sent by the Creator to watch over us? Is that all?"

"Nope," Klev chuckled. "Just the start of it. They easily live for a dozen human lives, and even so are barely considered middle-aged. They speak to animals, and the animals speak back. And each possesses a power—they call them blessings—that enable them great and fantastical abilities. And, perhaps more strangely, they only eat plants."

"Only plants?" Byrn repeated. "Like cattle?"

"No, like . . . spinach," Klev responded. "And they can sense how we feel inside. They like us to call them elves." Klev paused, gauging how Byrn was taking the information.

"Elves and Dwarves," Byrn's tone was incredulous. "My father was friends with magic elves who look like people, and a hidden family of Dwarves who actually are people. And he never mentioned either. And you expect me to believe this."

Klev's face showed no reaction to her comments, a fact Byrn found infuriating in itself. "I don't expect you to do anything. But if you are at all your father's daughter, then you know I speak the truth."

Byrn bristled at the man's bluntness. He was right, of course. She had always had a talent for knowing when a man spoke the truth, as had her father. It was one reason she had taken Fisk at his word when he promised to kill her. And it was the reason why, if this man could look her in the eyes and tell her of magic elves, then she was certain it must be true.

"This is absurd," Byrn stated, more to herself than to Klev.

"Perhaps," Klev responded. "But true. Generations ago, my family assisted people with their problems, for hire. One very strange day we were approached by the elves, who offered us an opportunity. They asked us to run a spy network, and also to provide protection and security to the King. Their only condition was complete secrecy. The King uses us as he will, but he knows we truly report to the elves."

"These—*elves*—are revealed only to your family, and to the King," Byrn stated, and Klev nodded in response. "And my father knew." Again, he nodded. "And you have not yet told my brother about yourselves or about the elves, though I suspect you are bound to do so."

Klev smiled like a proud instructor. "My dear, we were elated when we confirmed you were alive. Somehow you slipped past Riverbend's boundaries before we could find you, and we have been looking for you since. We thought it best to confirm our suspicions before we did anything rash. And you are almost correct. We are not bound to reveal anything to anyone. We take oaths of service, but those oaths are always given freely. No creature, man, or elf will ever bind us."

Byrn leaned forward, still finding it difficult to believe what she was hearing. *A secret spy network, run by magical elves right under my nose. And I never knew?* "And this deal offered by the elves—what did they provide you in return?"

Klev looked confused. "In return? Why, the opportunity to serve, and protect our land. To watch for threats to prosperity and peace, and help prevent them before they occur.

"They provide us the finances to stay comfortable as well." He waved his arm around the cave. "And they offered us these tunnels. They were built by the early Church here in Stonecrop, but long-forgotten to any except the elves. Now my family lives and works here, from our oldest to the youngest. And we all carry the surname Dwarve." Klev's eyes shone with pride. "The name is a badge of honor."

Byrn closed her eyes. When she opened them again the man who believed in elves was still there, not a trace of deception on his face. "And my father knew that his spy network was run by elves? Elves who talk to animals and hold magic powers?" Byrn shook her head as if trying not to hear her own words.

"He did. It brought him great comfort, actually."

"And they are here now, waiting to speak to me?" Byrn's eyes flicked around the room.

"They do want to speak to you, but they are not here now. Poor timing on their part, I'd say. But, regardless, one is on his way. He is a younger elf, not one we have seen often. But he strikes us well."

Byrn had no room left for surprise when she was escorted to a beautiful underground room and found her locked trunk was there, resting securely on a bench. She opened the chest, retrieved her notebook, and began to write.

Tann stood patiently in the elegant sun-lit room, listening as Eldest Kwabena, the elven leader, relayed the details of his assignment.

Tann had suspected he might be called to assist once he had heard about the situation with the humans. The potential for violence had escalated, and the elves thought it time to step in and protect the humans from further harm. Tann disliked the thought of war as much as any elf, but certainly there was someone more fit to assist than a shy young elf who, truth be told, preferred the labor of woodworking to the duties of being a protector.

So Tann had spent the morning wandering in the depths of the forest surrounding the elven village, as if one could hide from the Eldest. Though, he mused with some satisfaction, the secretarius had seemed particularly annoyed having to trek into the woods to deliver the summons. Being the personal assistant to the elven leader sometimes caused the secretarius to forget he was not the Eldest himself. Tann had tried not to grin as the man approached.

"Tuere viam, Tangatamanu Skycaller. You are summoned to attend Eldest Kwabena immediately." The secretarius had nodded curtly then stormed off without waiting for a reply.

Tann twirled a small stick in his fingers, and then snapped it in two. Once summoned, Tann knew there was nothing else but to go. So, here he stood, as Eldest Kwabena told him that he was to go to the human city of Stonecrop, far to the northeast. There he would meet with the human spy network known as the Dwarves, and prevent the outbreak of violence before it began.

He didn't enjoy the idea of traveling so far from the mountains, and found the protection of humans particularly confounding, as they seemed to get along well enough on their own. But in proper deference to his leader, he tried to keep his thoughts from his face. By the Eldest's return expression, he knew it wasn't working.

If Tann had nearly any other creature's blessing, he could have spent his life here in the elven village. Most elves eagerly sought assignments as their opportunities to serve the creatures of Fayen. But Tann believed there were other ways to serve. If he had his choice he would have become a woodworker, building and repairing the simple but elegant dwellings where the elves lived when they were not out on missions. Someone had to take care of things at home, and Tann thought there was a certain honor to it that the other elves didn't appreciate.

However, a life in the village was not a realistic goal for Tann. With the blessing of the perching birds, he could communicate with other elves over long distances. There were some tricks to it, but this ability made the perchers—as they were called—ideal for orchestrating the spy network.

It was actually one of the more common elven blessings, and so normally Tann managed to get away with letting the older perchers tend to business. But now, by coincidence, they were all away on other missions. And that was before a landslide in the southern jungles had caused a territory conflict between several gorilla troops. Things at that time having been quiet with the humans, Sabi, the percher who had been taking a shift at Stonecrop, had offered to assist.

As the only percher left in the village, Tann knew there was nothing preventing him from being sent as the one to prevent the human war. Once in Stonecrop, he could send reports back easily to the Eldest, without any messengers required. But still, Tann couldn't help shifting back and forth, the discomfort breaking through on his face.

Eldest Kwabena tapped his sandal impatiently on the intricately tiled floor. "It is the way of the perchers, friend. Your reluctance confuses me." Kwabena whisked his robes behind him, as the secretarius handed him a cup of tea before slipping from the room. Kwabena sipped delicately from the tiny cup. He stretched his lips out in front, as if to keep the hot brim away from his face.

Watching the Eldest drink his tea, Tann wondered if a break from the village might not be so bad after all. It was, as the Dwarves would say, a double-edged sword staying here with the other elves. It was a true paradise, one where he didn't have to help manage a bunch of grumpy humans or wade through a jungle with a troop of gorillas and their resident odors. On the other hand, being within constant reach of the Council and their freehanded sanctions could be equally as oppressive. *Maybe I should welcome a reason to get away for a bit. Creator's stockings that I never drink tea that way.*

"Eldest Kwabena, I display no reluctance. I welcome the opportunity to serve."

Kwabena sighed. "What makes the percher so flightly?"

Tann did not respond. He had learned long ago that when a council member, especially the Eldest, started to muse, it was best to stay out of it.

"You are all this way, impossible to pin down. For a group who could speak to me any moment at will, I have not yet heard from the others since our last communication, with which you assisted."

"Eldest, they are all working important tasks; they are likely distracted, and far from here. It is against protocol for me to reach out to them without great need, as they are mostly elder to me. And as you remember, the situation with the gorillas should soon be over, and I'm sure that Sabi will soon be available to—"

Kwabena flung his hand impatiently, somehow managing to not spill a single drop of the tea. Tann raised his eyebrows appreciatively as the Eldest again spoke. "Skycaller, I have no patience for this. I have no idea when friend Sabi will return, and I'll bet the Spire's peak that you already tried to contact her. Meanwhile, the humans are rapidly building two armies, each set on destroying the other. While I always hesitate to interfere in the dealings of humans, we cannot simply let them annihilate one another."

Tann looked with sympathy at the Eldest. He was under a great deal of strain these days. In his lifetime, he had seen relations with the humans fall apart, to the point where the protectors no longer revealed their existence to them other than by exception. He likely blamed the impending human war on his own failed policies, and it was clear by his gaunt face and wandering expressions that the thought of thousands of humans being needlessly slaughtered under his watch had been keeping him up at night.

In addition, there was the other worry. The one no elf discussed. It had been twenty-three years since the last placement, the elven equivalent of birth. Three years without a placement, even five years, this happened at times, just as some years were ripe with the placement of new elves. But nearly a quarter century had now passed, and the lack of new elven protectors was likely weighing on the Eldest's thoughts at least as much as the human conflict. Not for the pause itself, but the suggestion that the elves had displeased the Creator somehow, or that something—perhaps with nature itself—had gone amiss.

And all of this aside, Kwabena was correct as always. Tann *had* tried to contact Sabi, as well as several of the other perchers, but they had all ignored him. It's not that he blamed them. Communication over long distances was exhausting, and usually only done with consideration of the need. Over the last century or so, the perchers had developed a habit of being more selective in responding to communications from the others. It was not personal to this Eldest, though perhaps he thought it was. Either way, Kwabena must feel like he was losing control, in so many ways.

Tann held himself still, and tried to regain a somewhat appropriate demeanor. This was the Eldest, after all. He would do well to remember it. "Eldest, I apologize for my hesitation. I am happy to assist; please continue."

Kwabena's face relaxed, just a bit. "After his father's death, the new human King is using force to ensure his authority is unquestioned. Not so uncommon, except that he has taken it too far, and another group has formed an army to oppose him. We fear that neither side will back down, and, with the right sort of provocation, we may see a full-scale war that could be long and bloody if it is allowed to begin.

"Your spies have tried the normal methods to influence the leaders, but they are making no progress. But we think there may be another option. The human princess is alive. Her father was well-loved, and perhaps if we can put her into power, the people will forget the bad about her brother, and instead remember what they loved about her parents. Perhaps they will rally behind her, and she can sway the people to choose a path of peace.

"This princess is young and would have many years left to rule, by human standards, enough time for things to settle. She is currently an involuntary guest of your spy network, in the catacombs."

Kwabena paused to look at Tann. "Without a percher on hand, these messages take too long to reach me and are often garbled by the perception of the creature that brings them. And gone are the days when I can carry them myself." The Eldest gazed across the room wistfully, his voice trailing. When he resumed, he spoke again with confidence, his tone commanding.

"I need you to travel there, to Stonecrop. Talk to her, and devise a way to prevent the war. Let me know whether you make progress, or what other assistance you need. Then you may return if you wish. I am certain the other perchers can continue to run the network without you, once I am able to locate them." Kwabena's mouth tightened.

Tann had more questions to ask, but another glance at the Eldest's face stayed his words. "Do not worry, Eldest. The situation will be resolved. Sleep well."

Kwabena's eyes remained sad, though his expression softened. "It is best to remember something. Time carries on like the greatest of rivers, and someday even the highest of banks are washed back into its flow. I never believed that I, a simple Bovidae, would be Eldest. Yet here I am with the well-being of Fayen resting on my limited wisdom and vast impatience. For now, you may leave the network in other hands, but, someday, time may call you as well. Tuere viam, friend Tangatamanu."

Without further explanation, the Eldest disappeared through a flowing wall of loose fabric into his sleeping chamber, a sign Tann took to mean that the conversation was done.

Within a day of her arrival to the caves, Byrn wrote a letter to Dot, apologizing for leaving so suddenly but thanking her for her kindness and assuring her that she was well. She had also arranged for one of the Dwarves, posing as a wealthy traveler, to leave Dot an extravagantly generous tip, enough that Dot could hire someone else, for a while at least, and keep her sore wrists from worsening.

Despite no longer having to scrub pots in Dot's kitchen, Byrn's days were not idle. She was startled to find that the Dwarves expected her to take classes while they waited for the elven protector to arrive. A bit of her upbringing returning, she initially protested. "I have had greater instructors and more training than anyone my age. Do you forget who I am?"

Rather than bow or scrape, the Dwarves simply laughed. "If you were not who you were, we would not offer you such an opportunity."

Byrn quickly relented. The instructors were of higher quality than even her father's own staff, and she found the studies fascinating. They also met daily to discuss the escalation between King Fisk and the Merchants' Guild.

Fisk had the Royal Army at his disposal. Most of his forces remained gathered in the barracks outside of Riverbend Fortress, but others had been dispatched in smaller groups into Ellena itself. They were sent to enforce the new tariffs and trade regulations, but without any evidence the King really cared what they did, several of these groups had taken to terrorizing the local people, all in the name of justice and order.

The stories quickly reached Stonecrop of people being beheaded in the public square simply for refusing to be searched by the city guards. Fisk's forces had also assaulted several peaceful groups of traders traveling from Stonecrop down the Royal River. The presumption was that anyone taking that route, without the appropriate papers, intended to join the army of traitors, as they called it. The lucky ones escaped without their possessions in hand, while some others were wounded or even killed. One well-established merchant had chosen to speak publicly against the King, and his family—even his children—had been murdered in broad daylight and left where everyone could see them.

Byrn shuddered. "He believes that if he scares them enough, the people of the city will urge the Merchants' Guild to disband their army and simply follow his new policies. It is no longer a rightful monarchy; it is a tyranny." She ran her finger along the map spread across the thick wooden table. "Fisk will not back down; I am certain of it. And the Royal Army will remain loyal; they swore in their own blood to uphold the throne. So either the Guild gives in, which I doubt, or it becomes simply an issue of which army strikes first."

Klev nodded slowly. "Byrn, would you like a warmed mug of mead? These stories, I know they are difficult to hear." Byrn's face felt warm. She had tried to maintain a royal demeanor as the reports came in, but Klev seemed to have seen through it. An image flashed in her mind of the tiny innocent children, left dead in the center of the market to be covered in insects as people hurried by. She fought back a wave of nausea.

Byrn stared at him. "Have you approached him? I presume that you have." Even Klev nearly jumped at Byrn's piercing expression.

"Well that doesn't answer my question, but of course we have. Our agents are well-positioned, though not directly at his side. We tried to provide him multiple avenues to peace, but he is set on establishing his authority. He has no concern regarding the potential for war. If it comes to that, he believes it will solidify his rule, establish him as a warrior king, and bring any remaining doubters to his side, either through fear or admiration."

"Fisk would not care which," Byrn mumbled.

"No, he would not." Klev paused. "You do not ask the more important question, whether we have consulted with the Church."

Byrn was embarrassed she had not thought to ask. Being from Riverbend Fortress, she was used to people deferring only to the throne. She scolded herself for forgetting that here, in Stonecrop, the Church was a more widely-regarded authority even than her own family. *Of course, we can look to the Church.* "Yes of course, what did they say?"

Klev grunted. "They say politics are the choices of man, and it is not their place to become involved, only to provide comfort and spiritual guidance to all in troubled times."

Byrn grimaced. There was actually some comfort in their neutrality, but yet she decided to take Klev up on his offer of mead.

A few days later, Byrn was called to a room on a matter they told her was of a private nature. A year ago, Byrn would have never have tolerated the idea of being summoned anywhere, but the weeks spent waiting tables, and the continued reality that she was technically a prisoner, had desensitized her enough to prevent any indignant responses on the subject.

A woman held a door for her then walked quickly away. Byrn stepped into the room, to see a man leaning over a writing desk, his head in his hands. She withheld a gasp. "Lord Steward. I am thrilled that you are well."

"I am not well, girl. I failed you, failed your father. But what could I have done when he refused to change? Refused to listen? Killed the boy? I mean, I would have had I received those orders, but it was not my call to make. So I left. Ran away. Left you there, to fend for yourself. I was a coward."

Byrn welled with sympathy. A loyal soldier does not issue his own orders; this man had acted admirably. But, yet, she could imagine how he felt now, hearing the same stories that replayed over and over in her own mind, and knowing he could have prevented them. "You are a Dwarve?" But it was not really a question; it made sense.

"Yes." The Steward looked away, and Byrn understood. Spying on the King was treason. She could have him executed on the spot. But then, her father had probably known. Either way, it was not her concern.

She rested a hand on his shoulder. "You were a good and faithful Steward. What has happened is not your fault."

"Not entirely." The man continued to stare at the wall. "Your mother saw it, you know. Saw the hunger in his eyes as he grew increasingly distant. She cried herself to sleep many nights, at a loss of how to reach him. But she tried. Do you remember when they traveled to Atla together?"

Byrn hesitated; she had been much younger. But she did remember. "My mother returned to the fortress without Fisk. She told us that she was weary from the long journey, and had decided to take an early leave."

The Steward nodded, still not looking in Byrn's direction. "She hoped the time together would shape him. She tried to talk to him, to show him the man he needed to become. He called her cruel names, and sent her home. I will not repeat his words, but he said things to her a mother should never hear."

The Steward clenched his fists. "That foul—" He stopped, too upset to continue.

Byrn bristled at the revelation. She had not known. "How could he order her home?" Byrn whispered. "She was the Queen."

"She was. But your father's illness had already started to develop, and Fisk was young, ruthless, and the soldiers knew he might soon be their King. They feared your brother, feared what he could do to them if they disobeyed."

"My mother died not long after that trip."

"It was a sudden condition that took her, shortly after she returned to Riverbend. She had coughing fits that kept her up night after night. I am not suggesting Fisk had a role in it. But her heart was broken; she had no strength to fight. And she insisted you be kept away, for fear you would be stricken as well. And so she struggled for breath, heartbroken and alone. It was too much for her."

"And my father?" Byrn wasn't sure she wanted to hear the answer. Her father had been devastated after her mother's death. As his health worsened, year after year, he had often indicated that he had not done enough. He thought she would be fine, and just needed some rest and care. A weight settled in Byrn's chest. *Perhaps if I had stayed with her, she would be here today.*

The Steward's response interrupted her thoughts. "He should have dealt with Fisk. But picture him in your mind; he has your mother's face. When your father looked into Fisk's eyes, he only saw your mother. How could he do what must be done, with the eyes of his lost love staring back at him? And thus he did not step in, did not shape Fisk as he could have. Though," the Steward added sadly, "by then I suspect it was too late."

Byrn placed a hand on the man's shoulder. "What Fisk became was not your fault. You could not have challenged him alone. If you had confronted him, he would have had you killed, and you would not have been there all those years, to teach me. My mother spoke to me of your kindness. She frequently said we were fortunate to have you in our service, and that I could trust you. So much of what I know today comes from what I have learned from you."

He looked up at her gratefully, his eyes red. "You should be Queen."

Her smile was warm but for the concern in her eyes. "You can help me, as you helped my father."

But the man merely shook his head, before throwing it back into his hands.

Byrn stayed for a while, tidying the Steward's room, arranging his few trinkets, and ensuring that the pillows were fresh and soft. She told stories of her recent training as she set fresh flowers into a vase, and waited for the Steward to respond. But when it became clear he had no more to say, Byrn slipped back out into the passageway.

Only then did she allow the tears to flow.

Tann rested his hand on Takka's back. "You must be very tired. Are you sure we can't rest a day or two?"

Your Eldest has been good to my herd for many generations. I could not refuse any request, even one to carry a talks-too-much protector swiftly to the great river. And no, we won't rest more than we need to. Best to get you off my back sooner, if you will.

Tann grinned. He loved the mountain pronghorns. They were tough and practical, yet had a delightful sense of humor once you came to know them. Not all pronghorns could carry an elf while maintaining any speed or distance, but Takka was large, and Tann was among the smaller of the elves. Still, the creature must be tiring after the long journey from the mountains. Fortunately, they were almost to the River. Once there, he could send Takka on his way and simply hire a private boat to travel the rest of the way to Stonecrop.

When they reached the river, the parting was brief. Takka wished Tann continued safety, then bounded away toward the South. Another reason he loved the pronghorns—they never seemed to worry.

Tann had some experience with human ways, and catching a vessel was no issue at all. He drew no suspicion, being nearly of human size himself, and knowing how to dress as a common traveler. He never saw the value in drawing unnecessary attention, and secretly preferred the human style of dress to the lofty, garish robes of his own kind. *Whoever invented robes never rode a pronghorn,* he chuckled to himself.

It was twilight when Tann reached one of the secret entrances to the caves. He slipped inside, knowing that he was expected and thus would not trigger any security precautions or alarms.

The girl was waiting for him at a long table in the main hall. Though she was busying herself repairing the bindings on a stack of old books, clearly they had told her he was arriving. He smiled at seeing the books stacked across the table. It was the sort of task a new initiate would be trained to undertake. While it might seem to be menial work for a princess, it showed that the Dwarves held her in higher regard than she probably realized.

"Your Highness, it is a pleasure to meet you. I am Tangatamanu Skycaller, Protector of Fayen ex Passeriformes."

Byrn liked the elf immediately. It was hard for her to imagine that he was the magical being they had described, yet she knew it to be true. His demeanor was kind and relaxed, yet his eyes held a wisdom she had never seen in the expression of a man. She could even believe that he had lived more than three and a half centuries, as the others had told her. And yet, he was somehow still entirely normal.

A childhood spent in the castle at Riverbend Fortress made her always turn first to protocol. "I am Byrn, daughter of Korta, exiled Princess of Riverbend Fortress, and sister to the King, ruler of all Fayen. I am not familiar with the ways of protectors, please assist me in understanding how I shall address you."

Tann always found it curious how human leaders took on nearly as much ceremony as the elven leaders themselves. But Tann was never one for formality. He found it completely unnecessary, and he only cared for things that served a purpose.

"I propose that I will call you Byrn, and you will call me Tann. That's easy enough that even I'll remember it."

Byrn grinned at the unexpected response. "Well, Tann, it is an honor to meet you. Truly. But I suspect you did not come all the way here for an evening tea."

"I'd adore an evening tea, actually. A great idea." A woman behind him muttered something before turning back into the kitchen. "But, no, I am here because we are concerned about the prospect of war, and the impact it may have on humankind."

Byrn's expression shifted, her smile fading. "Over the course of my father's illness, the people became disconnected from my family. Without my father traveling the land, the people had no explanation for what were necessary policies. Reasonable tariffs became seen as burdens, and the people of both city and town grew tired of the regulations.

"Our choice of residence at Riverbend Fortress was intended to provide convenient travel to the various locations of the North. But once my father took to his bed, it served only to keep everyone at a distance from my family. I now understand what I did not before: that it was only an uncertain affection for my father—and perhaps also my mother—that had kept their disillusionment, their aggressions even, in check.

"Fisk's immediate priority should have been to calm the masses, to walk the streets listening to their grievances. To extend his hand and experience their suffering, whether real or perceived. While not all can be resolved by intervention of the crown, a swift ear blocks a thousand swords."

Tann's eyes sparkled. He had known and admired the elf that had coined that expression among the humans, though it was long before the lifetime of Byrn, or her father. It was touching that it survived. Not noticing Tann's expression, Byrn continued.

"Rather than calm their fears after my father's death, Fisk moved to ensure they knew a new King was their ruler now. He raised the tariffs and imposed additional regulations on trade. When those activities proved unpopular, he executed those who spoke up against the crown. When the executions led to protests, he restricted activities of gathering. When the Guild began to recruit their own forces, Fisk extended the conditions of Royal military service. He did these things by decree, without even a speech to explain his decisions. And so it continues to escalate.

"Normally discontent takes time to grow, but the people were a hopping kettle ready to boil over. The Merchants' Guild has formally declared a revolution. And now, they plan to march on the throne, kill the King, and take over rule of Fayen."

Tann always found such human statements interesting. Only humans presumed to rule all creatures, equating rule of their kind with rule of all. But he could not fault them, either. Without knowledge of the creatures hidden in the mountains, and without the ability to communicate directly with other species, perhaps they felt a unique responsibility that others would not understand.

The tea was soon delivered, and Tann drank it slowly as Byrn continued to talk. Tann only half-listened. He knew most of this already of course, but didn't want to be rude to the earnest young woman in front of him. What it all amounted to was that two armies gathered for war, and he had to figure out how a simple elf and a young human could possibly stop them.

Tann watched Byrn as she spoke. It was evident that she had grown up around rulers. She held her head high, made direct eye contact, and exuded an air of expectation that everyone would follow her every word. And Tann could sense her emotions, as he could the emotions of all creatures. She was calm and unafraid, even in his presence. Yes, she had the demeanor of one who could be Queen.

But there was something different as well. Even as she spoke, she continued to repair the damaged books in front of her. She opened each book, assessing its condition and pressing warm stones against the pages to smooth them. With careful precision, she spread a paste into areas that had separated before moving each book to her other side.

She worked diligently as she talked, portraying no sense that the task was beneath her. Tann tried to imagine Eldest Kwabena busy at work as he spoke, but it was an image he couldn't even conjure. Yet even the Eldest must have lived a normal life, working as others did. Tann wondered for the first time what Kwabena had been like in his younger days. It was not a thought he had considered before.

When Byrn finished talking, Tann set down his empty cup. "You should really try the tea. It is marvelously spiced, and not over-brewed. Now, let's discuss our plan."

Part III: The Night Raid

Tann, Byrn, and a pair of armed Dwarves—a man named Kee and a woman named Megh—set course for Ellena to attempt a meeting with the Merchants' Guild. With access to fast horses and the Dwarves' knowledge of the terrain, the journey from Stonecrop to Ellena was only days. Byrn tried not to let this bother her, remembering the length of time it had taken her to travel half as far through the forest on foot.

Tann talked to the four horses nearly as much as he did the three humans, a fact Byrn found unsettling, at least for a time, until she got used to it. She was excited to be making the trip. First, it was nice to be back out into the sunlight after being confined within the caves. Second, she had always enjoyed visiting Ellena. While she preferred the more traditional ways of Stonecrop, Ellena had a vibrant culture and spirit that she found unique and compelling.

She now sat patiently behind a wall—Tann, Kee, and Megh with her—waiting for someone who Tann was certain would return. Byrn looked over in surprise as a dog came bounding around the wall and approached Tann, whimpering in what sounded like a very ordinary way. But only Tann could hear the dog's words: *The whole guild is meeting tonight, as you thought. They ate already, and have had some wine. About as happy as they'll be, I'd say.*

"Thanks, Anni," Tann whispered, petting the dog's neck.

Byrn understood by Tann's response that the dog had been talking to Tann. She stared at the animal with a new interest. The dog tilted her head in Byrn's direction, and startled, Byrn nodded back.

Following the dog's lead, they moved forward to knock on the simple wooden door that was the true meeting place of the Merchants' Guild despite the garish brass sign across town. A woman peeked through a slot in the door, looking curiously at the small group in front of her.

"Buttons, what are you doing outside?" The woman glared down at the large dog, who was sitting with the strangers and slapping her tail enthusiastically from side to side.

"We have returned your dog to you, of course. I suggest you let us in on that premise, before I say anything publicly that could be more revealing." Tann stopped, waiting for the woman's response.

She peered out of the small flap in the door. Tann hoped that she would assess that whatever their intentions, four people alone could be dealt with securely. Apparently she did, as the door clicked, then swung open.

"In, now. Do as I say or we'll load you into a batch of foldover filling. Don't think we haven't or we won't."

Tann held back a chuckle. While the Merchants' Guild was sometimes known for being unforgiving and occasionally violent, he had a sharp nose for kindness and knew this woman wouldn't hurt a pepperfly if she didn't have to. "There will be no threat from us. We only wish to speak to the dinner party and we'll be quickly on our way."

She pointed at Kee and Megh, now seeing them more clearly. "These two, with the crossbows, they wait outside."

Tann nodded at the Dwarves. "We'll be alright. Wait outside, please."

The Dwarves' faces looked pained, but they stepped back through the door before it was again closed and locked. The woman led Tann and Byrn down a long hallway, as the dog walked closely at her side. Tann leaned toward her and whispered, "The dog, she prefers the name Anni. I have a way with dogs; you should trust me." The woman looked at Tann as though he were crazy, but before she could respond they had reached the dining hall, and neither the woman nor her dog followed them as Byrn and Tann stepped briskly into the large room.

A man stood up behind the table as they entered. Tann did not wait to speak. "We are not enemies, and we do not bear arms. Our guards wait outside, where they cannot reach us. We will not harm anyone, nor reveal your location or identities. We only wish to speak, and we will leave as quickly as we came."

The man sat down, though hesitantly. "Who are you?"

Tann turned toward Byrn, who stepped forward. The men looked at her skeptically.

"I am Byrn, formerly Princess Byrn of Riverbend Fortress, daughter of Korta, sister of the King."

Some of the men leaned back, and in the silence the chair backs creaked, as if also surprised. Byrn understood. Normally the mention of a King among his enemies would mean immediate imprisonment or worse. But Fisk had declared her dead with a childish tale that nobody had believed. If she really was the princess, it was not likely she was in league with Fisk.

A large man with a thick beard leaned forward, and began to speak. "Interesting idea. But if you don't mind my candor, you don't look like a princess." His eyes sauntered up and down her dress, then rested a long moment on her face.

Byrn suppressed her reaction, and instead responded calmly, as if the man were a noble, despite his insulting remarks and the shred of chicken hanging from his beard. "Perhaps your expectations of princesses are unrealistic. No matter. I have something with me that should convince you."

The men glanced amongst each other, rolling their eyes, expecting her to produce a jewel or even a crown. It was a common thing among families of wealth: to purchase something that looked of royal heritage. With such a thing, they could often rule the people of a small village, such people believing the extravagant trinkets as proof of royal blood. But the Merchants' Guild was run by shrewd and successful businessmen. A few grunted, as if it were beneath them to be the subject of such a ruse.

But when Byrn stepped forward she opened her hands, revealing a small piece of cloth. Now all the men leaned forward, to see what she held, for it was not jewelry nor coins, nor the great seal of a ruler. It was a baby's hat.

Several men gasped. To forge such a thing would be both nearly impossible as well as heretical. It was the blessing cap of a royal infant, woven over the course of many mooncycles by an Episcopus of the Cathedral, while in constant prayer for the well-being of the coming child. For very few was such a thing made. And when such a monarch or nobleman died, the cap was buried with them, as a reminder that all men remain children before the Creator.

A man whispered, "May I see it closer, Lady?" Byrn approached, holding the item toward him.

"You may not hold it; this would bring terrible misfortune on the man who touches it."

Several men nodded with great vigor. A merchant lived to trade, with one notable exception. Items of the Church could not be bartered, not under any circumstance. Such things belonged to the Creator, not to man. They did not know if reaching for an item would be seen the same way, but even for the men at the table of faded faith, they had no desire to take such a risk.

The merchants stared at the little hat, appreciating the item for its make as well as its rarity. It was woven in tiny intricate loops, intertwined with delicate stones of soft blue. The aquamarine stones, mined only in the remote islands of northern Fayen, were symbolic of the royal line. In the center was set a scarlet stone, of the color used to signify the Creator Himself, and in the shape of an oval, the symbol of creation. Several men turned their hand in the gesture of the oval, praying silently. Others began to bow.

The man in the center stood up abruptly, knocking over a glass, which tumbled to the floor, rattling until it hit the wall behind him. "Say we accept your little hat. What, then, do you want from us? To regain the throne? Because it's too late for that!" Through the closed door, a dog began to bark.

Byrn stood taller, a sense of her own royalty returning. She extended an arm in a gesture of openness. "I want peace and prosperity for our people. I want every man, woman, and child to wake up awaiting the warmth of sunrise, unafraid at what the light of day might bring. I want—"

"Get out!" The man swept his arm across the table, knocking several other dishes to the floor. Something broke with a loud crash. "Your poetry won't bring my son back, will it? Your blood, your status—it means nothing to me! It's hard work and compassion that make a man, not some blood tie to a sickly failure and his tyrant son. You are all the same! Power-hungry frauds, placating us with words, living your lavish lives on the backs of others! We do not need a King. We need a government, run by competent people who have done something with their lives other than spend the gold of their subjects!"

He sneered contemptuously at Byrn. "And you, Lady, have no qualification for anything other than being used as royal breeding stock." He peered at her suggestively. "And I can see why your brother has tried to keep us from that fate!"

Some of the other men started to laugh. Tann placed a warning arm on Byrn's arm. She shook it off.

"Your anger is understandable, but it is leading us to war. Can't you see that in battle, no man wins? Do you wish to see the blood of your kinsmen shed? Do you wish to see the—"

Several men rose threateningly from the table, and in the next moment Tann yanked Byrn by her arms and dragged her out of the building, pausing only to undo the bolt that held the outer door secure. Kee and Megh rushed to their side, and the four ran down several streets, turning frequently. When they finally stopped, Byrn pushed away Megh's steadying arms, and turned on Tann.

"Who do you think you are, laying your hands on a princess?"

"Simply your protector, Lady. And you can shout and holler all you want; it does not affect me. Those men, you almost swayed some of them. But their leader is too angry, and he was turning them against you. The dog, Anni, she told me that his guards were rushing down the hallway toward us. I had hoped these merchants would listen, but, well—we were losing control of the situation. I simply can't afford for you to be their prisoner, used as a bargaining chip against your brother."

"My brother does not care if I live or die!"

"Half-true, Byrn. He cares if you live."

Byrn caught herself; the elf was right on that point. She closed her eyes, and took a breath.

"Do we try again?"

"Not yet," Tann responded. "Let's return to Stonecrop, stay out of sight for a few days, and then we try the Duke."

The Duke of Stonecrop. Her father's cousin. She had nearly forgotten about him. She almost reached for her little bear, but remembered he was safe, locked away with her gold in the caves under Stonecrop. But the Duke—why had they heard nothing from him? Where was he? She looked back at Tann.

"The rumors, will they start that I am still alive?"

Tann grinned. "That is a certainty. I had hoped that we could negotiate a relationship with the merchants, but I knew that even if we failed, your revelation would not be kept secret. They will think it is a secret, of course, but one man will tell his wife. The wife will tell her friend. In turn, each will swear to keep the story secret, but with each the promise will weaken.

"Soon, your rumored survival will be spoken of on every street, every man swearing they heard the story from someone who saw you himself. Rumors started on the street fade with the wind, but a rumor started within the Guild itself will be a powerful thing. It is unclear when or if you can be revealed to the masses, but we must start them thinking you are alive if they are truly to accept it. And the little cap, it will seal the story's validity. It was wise of you to take it from the castle when you left."

Byrn nodded. Her training told her she should reproach the man for presuming to lead, but she forced herself to remember that he was an elf, not a man, and she had no throne from which to rule anyone.

With Kee's clever planning, the party slipped through the city limits without being caught by the merchants' security or stopped by one of Fisk's inspection teams. They headed back toward Stonecrop via the same route as before. Most travelers took the main road north until the river, catching a ferry to speed their journey from that point. But this route would have taken the small party past Riverbend Fortress, an area they all thought it best to avoid.

Instead they wove through the small farming communities of northern Fayen. On the horses, they made good time, and again it seemed the journey would only take a few days. They began to relax, and enjoy each other's company as they rode through the countryside.

The horses stopped suddenly at the bottom of a low hill, and Tann jumped down in alarm. "Someone coming this way," Tann whispered. "The horses can hear them."

No matter how friendly, she did not want to risk a meeting with anyone, especially on the off chance she would be recognized. Byrn glanced about, looking for a place to lead the horses. But now she could hear the approaching party as well. With little cover, there was no time to get out of sight without appearing suspicious.

"Back on your horse, Tann," she commanded.

Tann took no offense. His own songbirds argued with him constantly, and it was well understood among the elves that there was no creature more skeptical to the value of the elves' protection than the humans—one of the reasons the elves had generally given up on assisting them. Besides, what did Tann have to offer against a band of armed men? He jumped obediently back onto the horse, hoping the party would pass peacefully and soon be on their way.

Byrn grimaced. "Fisk's banner. Let me do the talking." Kee and Megh looked questioningly at Tann, who nodded and held a hand forward in caution. Byrn did not notice. "Tann, tell the horses to follow my lead." Byrn hesitated. "I'm sorry, ask them."

Tann nodded, and repeated Byrn's request to the horses. Byrn reached forward, placing a hand on the side of her horse's nose, and he nuzzled her back as if in understanding.

A group of six mounted men approached. They were all heavily armed, their bodies covered in studded leather armor, leaving only their faces exposed. Byrn knew that despite the two trained assassins at her side, Fisk's men would easily overpower them in combat. It could not come to that. The horse Byrn rode whinnied loudly, and one of the approaching horses seemed to respond. Tann nodded reassuringly at Byrn.

Kee whispered at Byrn's other side. "Probably a tariff inspection. Will also be searching for evidence that we are in league with the Guild. Most likely will rob us then send us on our way."

Byrn's response carried an edge to it. "Are you willing to take that risk? After I've just so recently come alive?"

Kee was at a loss for words, and Megh lowered her hand to her weapon. Tann sat quietly on his horse, and Byrn wondered what he was thinking. She felt bad for having snapped at Kee, but decided she would apologize after they were out of harm's way.

The men stopped some distance from Byrn and the others. "Announce yourselves," a man's voice boomed. "These roads are only traveled under orders of His Excellency, King Fisk of Fayen. Display your tariff papers."

Byrn spoke with a clear voice. "We were visiting friends in Ellena, and are now simply returning to our home. We do not travel on business, and carry nothing of value, and thus papers are not required." The two Dwarves tensed uncomfortably on their horses, though Tann remained impassive. Byrn felt uncertain, though it did not show in her voice or posture. The Steward had ensured she knew her own father's laws, but who knows what Fisk had done since. *Still, worth a try.*

"Ever'one needs papers now. King's order. Dismount, and place any weapons on the ground." Two of the men raised crossbows threateningly. "Do anything we don't like, and we'll just be done with you our way." One of the men bared his teeth menacingly.

The soldiers started moving toward the small group, the clip-clop of the large horses' hooves becoming louder against the small road. "I happen to know that it is a long walk back to Riverbend," Byrn stated quietly. She looked sideways at Tann, who whispered into his horse's ear. Tann nodded back at Byrn, who smiled appréciatively. Tann's horse neighed loudly.

Byrn waited until the horse was quiet, and raised a hand commandingly. "Be on your way. I am a noblewoman and do not consent to your search. Do not approach us further or you will regret the choice."

A couple of the men stopped, held in place by Byrn's confidence, looking nervously at one another.

The man in front laughed. With a quick flip of the reins, he moved rapidly toward Byrn's party, the others following. Byrn signaled to Tann. "Now!" Tann shouted.

The men's six horses changed course, violently bucking the men from their backs. The horses bolted to the side of the other four, and all took off at a gallop together, leaving the six soldiers on the ground behind. Two lay still, and three others rolled in pain. Another reached for his crossbow, and took aim as the ten horses galloped away. Byrn could hear the sharp crack of the crossbow, firing behind her.

Megh shouted in pain, and then became silent. Byrn looked over, to see Megh still atop her horse, her teeth gritted and face pale.

"You're hurt!" Byrn exclaimed.

"I'm fine," Megh growled. She reached down and pulled a bolt loose, throwing it to the ground behind them. "Let's get out of range and we'll deal with it. There is a town not far from here; they'll get new horses and be after us shortly." Byrn agreed reluctantly, and the group continued to ride.

After a bit, Byrn called out to Tann. "We have gone far enough. Tell them to stop."

"No," Megh insisted. "We aren't clear yet. A bit more."

Tann looked at Byrn's expression and decided not to push the issue. "All, let's hold for a minute." The horses slowed to a stop. Byrn and Kee pulled Megh down toward a soft patch of ground. Megh moaned, as they turned her over to inspect the wound.

"The bolt stuck right through the upper leg," Kee sighed. "She'll be fine, except she's losing too much blood." Kee stripped off his outer shirt, and did not object when Tann reached for it. "Your elven magic doesn't fix wounds, does it?"

"Only in legends, friend," Tann smiled. Taking his water flask, he wet the fabric and wrapped it tightly around Megh's thigh. After he had tied it off and inspected his work carefully, he patted her just above the wound. "You're lucky. Any higher, and you'd be really bummed." Tann's eyes twinkled. "Especially when it took us so long to stop."

"*What?*" Megh laughed.

"I mean to say, your horse might have reared at the shock," Tann stated, a serious expression on his face. "So I can imagine."

Megh laughed uncontrollably through the searing pain in her leg.

"Now, now—I'm sorry, dear; this is really no time to crack jokes." He reached over and placed a steadying hand on Megh's arm.

"I don't understand. Is she ok?" Byrn stood over Megh and Tann, looking confused, as Kee stood to the side, trying to hide his snorts in a fit of coughing.

"Oh, nothing Byrn. Megh just thinks I am excessively cheeky for an elf. *But* she's wrong." Megh picked up a small rock and threw it at Tann, who bounded out of its way with a wink.

Byrn looked between the others, laughing together, and shrugged. Convinced she had missed something, she was glad to see the others laughing, especially Megh.

Tann lifted Megh onto her mare, and then gracefully mounted his own horse without looking back in Byrn's direction. "One of the Dwarves told me laughter was the best medicine," he muttered, as Kee and Byrn hopped onto their horses. "Just thought I'd try it out."

Three of the additional horses asked to leave the group, comfortable living in the wild and tired of transporting humans. The others, caught in the excitement of meeting their first elven protector, asked to return to the Dwarves' stables, knowing they would be treated well and could decide later whether they wanted to stay in service or also leave for the wild.

Once back in Stonecrop, Megh's wound was cleaned properly, and Byrn was reassured she'd be back on her feet in a matter of days.

Byrn and Tann began planning a trip to visit the Duke. They took several days to scout the estate, having agreed that caution was necessary. The risk of meeting with the Duke was high enough without a chance of running into Fisk's men. But if the Duke proved to be an ally, he had many powerful friends. In addition, his estate would provide an above-ground base of operations, which could prove to be essential no matter how things went. And so they continued to gather information and make their plans.

They learned that the estate appeared to have been mostly abandoned, and it seemed—for some unknown reason—that Fisk wasn't even having it watched. But according to a blue jay who liked to sit on the Duke's windowsill, the Duke was rumored to still be inside.

Early one morning, Tann asked the Duke's cats to lead them to him, as the estate was known to be expansive. They cats agreed, though only after Tann agreed to scratch all of their ears, one after the other, in turn. Byrn glanced around impatiently as Tann moved down the line, scratching each cat's ears and dodging their nipping teeth, as they purred loudly. Once ready, they silently followed the cats down a series of hallways, then stopped in front of a set of double doors. Byrn took a calming breath, and then Tann let them in.

The Duke jumped from his chair, a large dagger in his hand. As he stood, he teetered unsteadily, grabbing the back of the chair to keep himself from falling forward. Byrn looked around with a heavy heart. The room smelled of mead mingled with a faint odor of urine. Clothes and linens were strewn about, the floors completely unswept, attracting insects and small mice, who scurried as they entered. There was no need of the infant cap, as the Duke recognized her immediately.

"Byrn! You're alive! Bless Creation!" He began to weep loudly, to Byrn's great discomfort. Even Tann looked confused.

"Where are your servants?" Byrn resisted the urge to hold her nose. The elderly man had, after all, always been kind to her.

"The King, er, your brother, he took them to Riverbend. Said I had no need of such luxuries. Told me to wait here until he had use for me."

Byrn almost asked the man why Fisk had not simply killed him. By the look on Tann's face he was wondering the same thing. She tried to lift the old man's spirits by speaking of hope, and peace, and the need to intervene when innocent life was threatened. She paused. The Duke was not listening.

"My Marta. He has my Marta. He said if I do anything other than sit here, then he'll hurt her."

Byrn winced. The Duke had married a much younger woman a few years back. It had seemed more of a vanity and there were no political implications, so she had forgotten. But Byrn understood better now: the monster had kidnapped the old man's wife, taken his servants from him, and left him to empty his own chamber pot after each night of tearful drinking.

It was clear to Byrn that the man was broken, and Byrn had little hope that the Duke's wife had even survived her first night. As there was no charade of a stable governor anyway, Tann and Byrn escorted the Duke back to the caves, and put him in an apartment next to the former Steward. Byrn and the others still had work to do, but perhaps the men could provide strength to each other.

Byrn returned to the Duke's estate alone that night with a mop and a bucket—well, nearly alone. Kee had insisted on accompanying her. "You'll never sneak out of here without a guide; our security is too good. I respect what you're going to do, so I'll guard you, but you need to understand the risk we're taking." Kee finished his lecture. "Er, your Highness." He bowed low.

Byrn laughed. "I'm not much of a leader, am I?"

Kee shook his head in earnest. "It's not true, actually. You're a fine leader. The way we talk around you, it's well—I'm sorry."

Byrn smiled. "As long as the scolding is in private, I am grateful to have friends like you. If I am ever Queen, I hope you'll be in my security detail."

"Oh, that'd be great," Kee smiled. "I mean, an honor, your Highness."

Byrn and Kee spent much of the night cleaning the Duke's quarters. "There," she said, surveying the room. She looked at Kee with concern.

"I won't say a word," he promised. Byrn clasped his hand gratefully.

Tann was waiting up in the common area when they returned, despite the late hour. Byrn smiled to herself. She had been told elves did not have families, yet Tann could be remarkably paternal. He watched as she put the mop and bucket back into a side nook, near the kitchen.

"We're fine, Tann."

"It was kind, what you did." Tann nearly knocked over a small teapot as he reached for it. He swore under his breath, a habit Byrn was certain he was picking up from the Dwarves. "I will tell him tomorrow that the nature of his condition has been contained to a few whom he can trust to keep it so. But, please, no more such risks. At least until matters are in hand." Byrn nodded, and gave the elf a quick hug before retiring to bed.

Tann sat alone in the common area, swirling the tea in his cup.

The ceremonial garden was a centerpiece of the elven village. Nestled into the heart of the western mountains, it housed plants and flowers native to all regions of Fayen. It was also Jeekra's favorite place to relax. An elf who appreciated his time alone, he tired quickly of the crowded paths of the elven village. Never losing sight of having access to the most beautifully tended garden in Fayen, he visited here frequently.

Today, he sat along the edge of his favorite fountain, one with a statue of a group of elves, all laughing. There were fountains scattered throughout the garden, each with a beautifully sculpted statue in the center. Most of the statues were serious or contemplative, and depicted elves conducting wise or benevolent acts. But this one showed laughter. It seemed inappropriate, somehow, against the decorum of the place, mismatched even against Jeekra's usually serious personality. But secretly it was his favorite.

He closed his eyes, and breathed in the beautiful scents of the garden. Lovely flowers mingled with grasses wafting in little sporadic breezes. Hearing soft footsteps behind him, he opened his eyes. "Good day, Rikian."

"Good day, friend Jeekra. I apologize for interrupting you but I happened to be passing by."

Jeekra doubted Rikian ever was just "passing by." He considered Rikian one of the more astute elves in Fayen, and one who was usually the first to know when anything of note occurred. "Rikian, I presume you heard about the Eldest's meeting with the lizards?"

Rikian sat on a nearby ledge, leaning to pet a tiny flower. "Not the specifics, but I'd love to hear more. Go on."

Jeekra smiled. He had always appreciated the eccentric elf, underestimated by others. Rikian was a Magnoliales elf. Magnolias, as they were called, could control the beauty of objects. Not generally considered helpful in the protection of Fayen's creatures, they often fell into aesthetic roles within the village, such as decorating new lodgings, making trinkets, or in Rikian's case, tending to the gardens. But Jeekra had always believed that dismissing any elf's blessing only demonstrated one's own limitations.

Jeekra's blessing was that of color and heat. The Squamata elves, known casually as lizards, were the counterpart to the spy network run by the perchers, like Tann. The perchers could communicate long-distance, making them excellent choices to run an intelligence network. The lizards could conceal themselves, and were resistant to difficult conditions of travel, making them perfectly suited for reconnaissance operations. Working in concert with the perchers, they were among the protectors' most powerful assets.

Which led to the reason Jeekra had come to the garden to relax: he needed to decompress after the meeting with Eldest Kwabena. Tann had provided the Eldest with updates on the most recent human conflict. Things were not going well, it seemed, and the normal arguments were not swaying the powerful parties among the humans.

Tann feared the imminent breakout of widespread violence, and while he said he was working to prevent or at least shorten it, he would need help if it came to a full-scale war. And when perchers needed help, they always turned to the lizards. At least that's how the lizards saw it.

Jeekra was not one of the senior lizards, but he was one of the more skilled. And so when the elven council convened, they had decided that he was the one who would go to assist. Once given an order, it was customary to be on your way by nightfall. But that didn't prevent a slight rest first. It was always good to clear the mind.

Instead, Jeekra found himself relaying the details of the meeting to Rikian, who paced about eagerly, occasionally asking questions. "So the humans march to war against each other over the rule of their cities. Now, tell me the sides again? What is the King called?"

"The King is called Fisk, and—" Jeekra began.

"How bucolic," Rikian interrupted.

"Please let me finish. King Fisk has access to his own Royal Army. And the other army is led by an organization of traders known as the Merchants' Guild, who are disillusioned with the King and want to overthrow him."

"And which side are we on?"

"Neither. Both groups are led by hard-headed fools wishing to destroy each other and everyone around them. We found another option, the King's younger sister. He told everyone she was dead, but apparently he let her slip off into the night with only a death threat, due to some twisted morality that enables him to kill nearly anyone who disagrees with him but provides him leniency toward his own kin."

"So then," Rikian said, opening both hands in a questioning gesture. "What has been the issue in establishing the girl as Queen? These are humans, right? Dress her up, show her assets, and march her around a bit. Should get their attention."

Jeekra laughed. "Well they did send Tann to assist, if that tells you anything. Never been much a student of attraction."

"No," Rikian agreed. "Nor attractiveness. Even for an elf, Tann wouldn't know style if a classic pattern walked into his hut and layered itself on top of a black sheer drape. Remember the time he called Elder Louvis's robes yellow?"

"What?"

"Never mind. My point is, as much as Tann purports to know human behavior, he forgets that they operate on the senses much more than they do on logic. They look like us, but they are not us. It's important to remember that." Rikian peered at Jeekra. "So what's your plan?"

"I don't have a plan," Jeekra responded. "But with Tann there to assist, the two of us will be sure to come up with something. They say Tann keeps to himself, but I have heard he is very clever. Especially given our affiliation, I have been thinking for a while I should get to know him better; perhaps this provides an opportunity."

"That's still not a plan." Rikian tapped the edge of the fountain softly.

"Rikian, are you trying to go with me?"

"Well, if you'd like me to, fine, but only because you asked. Let me go pack a few things and arrange for some transportation. Start walking toward the Spire; I'll meet you there." Rikian spun around and disappeared behind a row of hedges, out of Jeekra's sight.

Jeekra knew Rikian would have a reason for wanting to go with him, but would never in a million years confess to it. But Rikian was a good elf, and perhaps the company would be nice. It was a long journey to Stonecrop, after all. He felt a sense of amusement around him. He glanced down at the flowery vines, winding across the delicate arches behind the fountain. "Oh, stop it. It's not so funny as that."

Klev Dwarve's voice shook as he addressed the network, gathered together in the dining cave. People shivered in their sleeping gowns, but knew that Klev would not have roused them from sleep if the news were not important. Tann stood silently behind him.

"Brace yourself, my family. It is bad news." Klev took a deep breath, and he began. "It started two nights ago, in Ellena. It started as a raid on a stock of grain. The King had learned the Guild was keeping a huge amount hidden from his tariff inspectors, and wanted to teach the merchants a lesson." A rumbling moved through the crowd. Parents pulled their children tightly to their side.

"Fisk's men meant to start trouble, though perhaps not of this magnitude. To raid in the dark of night, with a band of armed soldiers—this is not how a simple inspection is conducted. And the Guild had guards outside the facility, who refused to let the soldiers in. As the commotion grew, townsfolk, craftsman, and families joined the gathering mob.

"Chants of protest grew. People first yelled about the raid, and about the tariffs, and their rights as citizens. Then someone started shouting, 'Death to the King' and that's when it started." Klev paused. "We don't know who attacked first. But when the violence erupted, it spread like fire. At first, the battle was between the mob and the soldiers."

No one spoke. Klev continued, "Imagine, armed mounted soldiers against unarmed families. It was a slaughter. And it didn't stop there. Enraged soldiers raced through the city, and even as they left, they cut down anyone who stood in their path. In their terror, some of the citizens rode outside of town to seek help from the Guild's army." Several people in the room gasped, but did not speak.

Klev nodded. "Yes, you can see where this goes. Members of the Guild's hired army rushed into town to defend the people, but the King's soldiers, their 'raid' complete, had already left. In their confusion, the citizens continued to fight, not realizing it was their own army they now opposed. Some of the soldiers got out, but others defended themselves against the attacks. Now, the battle continued. And the townsfolk saw the Guild banner instead of the King's as their friends died in front of them."

Klev tried to continue, but a woman interrupted him. "What sort of army was this, anyway?! Mercenaries and townsfolk led by merchants! To let armed soldiers into its midst, unchecked? They did not properly guard the city!"

"As if you could guard Ellena anyway," a large man growled from the back of the room. Around him, the others nodded in agreement. "We tried to tell them!"

Byrn had heard the Dwarves talk about this before. Unlike the tall fortress of Riverbend, where she had grown up, or the walled city of Stonecrop, where they currently resided, Ellena was a center of commerce and trade. It had grown from the trading post in the center of a large area of fertile farmland. As such, it was not surrounded by mountains, gullies, or other natural barriers. It was essentially impossible to defend against any serious attack.

Dwarves operating within the Guild had tried to plant this fear, but the Guild had been so set on marching toward Riverbend Fortress to depose the King, that they insisted the battle would occur there. They had already named it, "The Battle of Riverbend" and one man had even begun to write a long meandering song about it, much to the disgust of the Dwarves. But having maintained this vision of an epic clash between armies, the Guild never believed violence could erupt within the city. And now, the slaying of woman and children rested not just on the King, but on their own men.

The room drew silent, waiting to hear what else Klev had to say. "The fear I see in your eyes is founded. In the confusion, all civility was lost. Destruction and killing was random, brutal, and without mercy. Families were slain in their beds, their buildings burned to the ground. Others were left untouched. It was not a battle. It was . . . a massacre. And, no, we did not see this coming. Not yet." Klev's head bowed toward the floor.

Byrn knew that for a spymaster, it brought great shame to have missed the signs of an invasion into the city, even if the resulting conflict had been spontaneous. She was certain that Klev took the night's deaths personally. She hesitantly laid a hand on his shoulder. He did not react.

"There's more, isn't there?" Byrn whispered.

Klev nodded, and looked back up. He spoke loudly enough that all could hear. "The word was spread throughout the town that it was the Guild's forces that attacked in the first place. Others insist it was the King's doing. The people are divided, and fearful.

"One crowd gathered in the trade district, where the chants of, 'Death to the King' resumed. This crowd has rallied around the mercenary army, and is spreading word that their King is a murderer and a coward, and that the people have no choice except but to act. They insist that the formal siege on Riverbend must begin, that nothing but Fisk's death will return peace to the land.

"Another crowd gathered in the farmers' district, begging for the King to protect them. They spread the word that the King has promised riches and prosperity to his supporters in their war against the greedy merchants. They have declared that the merchants' only aim is to keep their riches to themselves, while the King wishes to spread the wealth of the land among the masses."

Byrn paused. "We met the merchants; they did not impress me."

Klev looked at her thoughtfully. "Rarely are those who clamor for power unblemished. It is a delicate game that enables people of motivation to stay in power, yet finds those motivated for the best reasons. There is never a perfect solution, only a never-ending struggle for balance. The night's events will inflame great passion, and move that point of balance even further out of reach. Nobody even knows which side they are on anymore."

Byrn stared at the torches burning on the walls of the spacious underground room. "I wish we didn't have to pick a side, that we could just work together." Klev did not respond. Around her children sniffled, and their parents as well, perhaps imaging what it would be like to see your family killed before you. *For no worthwhile reason.* "We can't let them go to war. These are my people."

"If war could be prevented by will alone, then there would never be a battle fought." Klev stood a little straighter, and now spoke in a whisper for Byrn's ears alone. "And, your Highness, despite our unyielding loyalty, you will lead us best when you learn we are our own people." Byrn's cheeks flushed, and Klev softened his tone. "But, still, Byrn—we'll try. Together."

Part IV: The Lady's Speech

"Tann! It is always such a pleasure to see you." Rikian bowed gracefully. Jeekra approached Tann with an arm extended. The Dwarves had reported the two elves approaching Stonecroft on foot, and Tann had decided it best to meet them outside the city walls, before they drew more attention than was prudent.

"Friends, so good to see you," Tann responded, nodding to Rikian and briefly grasping Jeekra's arm. "Now, let's get out of sight; you don't exactly blend in." Tann sighed. Though the arriving elves were not wearing traditional robes, still they wore robes rather than pants and a top, and Rikian's was a brilliant blue, of a color for which Tann was certain no dye was even found in nature. Tann would have to get the Dwarves to sew them some clothes if they were going to move about in public. "You arrived quickly. I am glad to see you are safe."

"Yes, we enlisted the help of a pair of exceedingly fast steeds." Rikian responded, nonchalantly. Jeekra's mouth broke into a very slight smile.

They got into a carriage and the curtains were quickly drawn around them. Rikian raised an eyebrow. "Yes," Tann responded, "The humans prefer that nobody sees where the entrances to the caves are if they don't have to. That includes us. The Dwarves are a secretive group, but it is also the way they stay so successful. I am starting to wonder what we'd do without them."

After a bit, the three elves entered the main hall, and were exchanging pleasantries with Klev. "So, you see, I am a bit of a casual gardener and occasional jeweler. And assuming you are successful in this endeavor, I wanted to make a perfect coronation ring for the new Queen," Rikian finished, before sampling a bit of the fried carrot strings the kitchen had prepared specially for their arrival. Dusted in ginger, they were simple, yet delicious. Rikian silently vowed to find whoever it was in the kitchen with such good taste and thank them personally.

That evening, the three elves met in a private room to discuss the situation. "It is not straightforward," Tann mused. "Normally we side with someone, and so have an ally to advance, and an adversary to block. But we are nowhere with either faction; we've simply made no strides with the King or the merchants. The merchants are blinded by justice, and the King by power. And add to it, we are simply out of time. They are preparing for a massive battle as we speak. We must act immediately."

"This lust for violence, I don't understand it," Jeekra stated. "With most creatures, they fight in defense, or over food, or a mate. Here, they clamor for war, for no gain that I can see."

"Oh, it's not so different, Jeekra," Tann responded. "The humans are just more complicated. Territory, wealth, freedom of activity—these are the things each side wants to control. It's all really shelter and food when you come to it. Not really so different."

"I don't know, Tann. Most creatures don't risk the well-being of an entire society over a conflict between a few."

"Well, I hadn't thought of it that way, but, yes, in that regard the humans are unique."

Rikian was wandering around the room, as Tann and Jeekra paused to watch. "Decorating?" Jeekra offered.

Rikian scowled. "Go ahead and laugh, but most elves spend their whole lives staring at the same few little trinkets. Why shouldn't ensuring those things are beautiful be a priority, when those objects pervade so much of our consciousness and otherwise? Besides, it helps me think."

Tann stood up to stretch, watching as Rikian reached out to touch an old woven tapestry on the wall. It depicted an elf in female robes, standing alongside a slightly awkward depiction of an elk. Immediately, the proportion of the scene shifted, and the colors became more vivid. The lighting in the scene adjusted, the sky less blue and more natural, with streaks of a subtle shade of lavender running through it. While it was basically the same scene, it was now, well, captivatingly beautiful.

Tann couldn't take his eyes from the adjusted tapestry. Whatever Rikian had just done made the whole image spring to life. "Well, hopefully that wasn't a sentimental piece."

Rikian's eyes rolled dismissively. "Everyone presumes to know me, yet I so often suspect that no one really knows me at all. I did, despite your insinuation, ask your little human friends permission to spruce up the room a bit. They said I could enhance anything within these walls; it was no issue to them. I took the agreement literally. And besides, did you see that elk? I understand that weaving is difficult work, but the elk's antlers were so lopsided he would be walking in circles. And if Clawstretcher ever saw that depiction of her face, she'd—"

"He's got a point, Tann," Jeekra interrupted. "But we were discussing the human war? Immediate need?"

Tann gave the tapestry a final glance. "Being on the wrong side of Clawstretcher is not something I think I'd enjoy. Perhaps it's better that she's been . . . resolved. A bit."

Rikian looked irritated at Jeekra's change of subject, but not for long. Jeekra had always been an especially close friend; their relationship was difficult to describe, but special enough to survive the occasional dismissal over subjects of style. Everyone criticized Rikian for being too superficial, but how else would one act, having the blessing of beauty? Their expectations were unreasonable.

Tann and Jeekra were back to discussing the conflict, as Rikian returned to touching up the room. After all, planning a strategy required inspiration. *Nobody appreciates such things!*

"Well, I think that's our best plan for now, then," Tann finished. "You scout the armies, influence them if you can, but at least learn how much time we have. Rikian will get to work on the Duke's estate, and fashion a proper palace for the girl. We'll need an appropriate balcony, with a bit of amplification built in. And I'll begin work on the speech."

"I'm sorry, I got distracted." Rikian sat back down at the table. "You want me to work on a setting for introducing our little princess?"

"Well, yes, I hope that's alright, Rikian. But when introducing a new leader to humans, the setting is important. We want them to believe—really believe—that she can be their Queen."

"Of course, Tann. And don't worry, I'll see to it."

Jeekra was a fast traveler, and it had taken him very little time to arrive at the outskirts of Ellena, where the Merchants' Guild had amassed a large army. He had been standing in the shadows of a large tree for most of the day, observing the patterns of activity and assessing what sort of people he had to deal with. From what he had heard, the leadership meeting would happen now, as the sun began to set. He began to move toward the main tent.

Jeekra concentrated on his blessing, and changing the color of his body and clothes, he blended into the background behind him. He became so integrated with his surroundings that he was nearly impossible to see. He couldn't hold this level of concealment for terribly long, but it should be plenty of time to attend the meeting, which he could see gathering in the tent ahead of him.

He slipped through the rows of soldiers, preparing to sleep. The men were not talking or laughing. Instead, they sat quietly smoking packed rolls of leaf, staring off blankly into the dark gray sky. Jeekra could sense the emotions of the men around him. They were sad, and emanated loneliness and hopelessness. It was clear no man here believed in this army, or in it having any purpose. Jeekra hesitated. It was beyond his ability to understand why they stayed, why they wouldn't just leave. What payment could justify such sorrow?

But he could not dwell on it; he was running out of time. He slipped past three rows of guards and in through the tent flap, just as they closed it. One man glanced suspiciously at the canvas door as it flapped shut with a small thud. But then he turned toward the others. "The attacks on our people can't be tolerated. Especially not when they're blaming us for it."

The men nodded in agreement. Another man waved a short sword in the air, "I'll lop off every one of their heads myself for what they did to us."

A younger man, polishing a line of boots in the back piped up, "Perhaps we'll need to find you a gentleman's sword, then, so you can return that one to your grandmammy." The man chortled, before growing serious again.

"If you met my Grammi, you'd say no such thing; I promise you that!" The man huffed in indignation, as others chuckled around him.

Jeekra felt a surge of anger. Though every elf claimed to have a solid understanding of the humans, few in these centuries had spent much time amongst them. So while the elves talked with a scholarly authority on the subject of human emotions, to see them in action was . . . disturbing. To laugh about killing someone they had never met? It was perverse.

Jeekra calmed himself. He must concentrate on his blessing, which modified his coloring, keeping him nearly perfectly camouflaged against the wall of the tent. He concentrated harder, as he could not risk the consequence of a large elf appearing suddenly in the middle of the leadership tent. The last time a lizard had made such an error, he had been worshipped for two centuries until the perchers could plant enough information to discredit the story. The perchers had never let that one drop, either. Jeekra grimaced.

Another man spit into the fire in the center of the tent. "They want blood, we'll give 'em blood." A few of the others growled in response.

"It's for our future, for our freedom."

"For our families!"

The first man to speak had been slowly drawing a picture of a crown into the dirt. Suddenly, he stuck his sword into the image, where it stood firmly, planted into the ground. The tent grew silent.

"I have my decision. We march now. It's war he wants; it's war he gets." The men cheered enthusiastically. "Lirr, how long to pack everything and be moving?"

"A few days to pack, a few days to arrive. Then we can set up and be ready when you make the call." The others nodded in agreement.

Jeekra drew back. *It's true, then. We are out of time.*

That night, Jeekra whispered in the man's ear. "Boss, you there?" The man grunted. "You know how everyone says Byrn is alive? You know, King's sister? Well there's some news going around. They say that the morning after the full moon, at midday, she'll be announcing a plan to overthrow the King. We ought to send someone, and just keep an eye on it."

"Yeah, we should. Go tell Venn, tell him I said so." The man rolled back over and was soon asleep, snoring loudly as the embers of the fire slowly turned the tent into darkness.

And so it was that Venn, the lead of the night watch, sent several of his best men and fastest horses that night, to ride to Stonecrop to hear the dead Princess speak.

Jeekra did not rest. He spent the night moving through the camp, whispering to men that the Princess was alive, and that she wanted peace for them and for their families. "The merchants," he whispered. "They cannot stop the true Queen. Not if you demand it."

Though tired, Jeekra pushed forward, riding north toward Riverbend Fortress, where he visited King Fisk's army the next night. Fisk was better guarded than the merchants were, but his officers were not. Jeekra, who had used his blessing to color his clothes like a royal uniform, moved through the barracks of the moderately-ranking officers, feeding rumors that the Princess was alive, and that her speech, on the morning after the full moon, would change history forever.

And so it was that the King's advisors sent their best men and fastest horses that night, to ride to Stonecrop to hear the dead Princess speak.

Jeekra returned, exhausted, to the little underground room, buried in the depths of Stonecrop. Tann read him a draft of the speech he had written. It was the speech of a lifetime, the one over which Tann had been poring for days: adjusting, editing, and scratching out entire sections before beginning anew.

"Well, that's it, then. What do you think?" Tann asked, but Jeekra was fast asleep.

It was the day after the full moon. The elves had accompanied Byrn to the Duke's estate, where, just behind a large set of curtains, they now stood waiting. The estate was now a sight indeed, with stone mosaics laid into beautiful patterns and elaborate tapestries hanging from the walls. Tann laughed, as only Rikian could have created such works of art so quickly. "How did you make all these things in such a short time?"

Rikian smiled. "It wasn't all me, you know. There are always artists in a city such as this, always clamoring for work or for recognition. I pulled some in, that's all. I just fixed things a bit when their work needed . . . enhancement. All part of the arrangement."

Byrn walked forward slowly, as several attendants made last minute adjustments to her hair and gown. Tann stepped closer. "I am afraid to touch you in that get up." Byrn giggled. "And I admit, I'm not as confident in the speech as I wish I could be. I revise and revise the words, just to find that I am further from what I want to say than when I started." He relaxed slightly, tapping Byrn playfully on the nose before being pulled away by her attendants.

"But I am confident in one thing: your ability to deliver it." Tann bowed deeply. "I will be honored to hear you, friend."

Byrn started to lurch forward as if to hug the elf, but the urgent tsking of a host of attendants stopped her. "Sorry, the dress. You know."

Tann laughed, as Jeekra approached, wringing his hands together. "We are losing control, despite our best efforts. The armies are already marching on each other, and will meet in combat soon. Your words, they will be critical, as will your poise. Stay focused, and let nothing they say or do sway your demeanor. We will be here, protecting you."

"Jeekra, set your worries aside. I have never felt so secure as with you and the Dwarves as my protection. I fear nothing today," Byrn said.

As Jeekra stepped back, Rikian approached Byrn. "My Lady, it has been an honor to get to know you. And what I have learned is that you are a creature of great potential." Rikian reached forward, and despite the warning murmurs of the attendants, held her hands softly, staring into her eyes. "You will be radiant. I am certain of it." Byrn felt faint for a moment, then steeled her nerves. Rikian stepped back, shaking a finger at the huffing women.

Byrn stepped onto the balcony. She gasped at the massive crowd gathered just below. The Dwarves had been very effective in bringing the people of Stonecrop here, as well as the prominent citizens of Ellena and also those of other towns and villages. Byrn wondered if representatives of the Merchants' Guild were there as well. She suspected they were, though probably in disguise, or with hoods drawn to hide their faces.

"Citizens of Fayen," she started. Her voice boomed out onto the street. Tann had warned her that the balcony had been modified to amplify her voice, but she had not been prepared for how effective the elves' work was. "You know me as Princess Byrn of Riverbend Fortress, daughter of Korta, and sister of the King. But I have taken a new palace here, in Stonecrop.

"For, you see, I cannot and will not take from you your rightful King. But it is proper, through the trust you have placed in my family for generations, that I establish a location from which to serve you. I will live here, as the Duchess of Stonecrop, and will hear your petitions. I will form a council of governors, who will act upon your needs, and ensure your rights as citizens are heard and respected."

The crowd began to buzz.

"It's her, isn't it?"

"I never knew she was so beautiful."

"It's really Byrn! Our princess!"

"Lovely, just like her mother."

"Her gown is so elegant."

The crowd quieted, straining to hear as Byrn continued. "I did not die on the eve of my father's death as you were told. I was forced from my home and denied my own name. But I did not leave you, citizens. I hid, and learned, and reached out to whoever would listen. Because this war, this violence that threatens your children, it cannot be allowed to continue."

An arrow whizzed through the air, sticking in the wall next to Byrn's head. She looked out at the crowd, and saw a man being dragged away by a pair of women, one of whom she recognized as Megh. The crowd noise grew, but Byrn continued to speak.

"Peace cannot be taken from us, not if we all choose it. One man, two men, or even a thousand cannot force war upon the entire land. Let us band together, as equals, and if we do—" Byrn paused for a long moment, as Tann had written into the speech, and then continued. "If we do—then our peace shall be immortal."

The crowd roared.

Listening to the cheers from below, Byrn now remembered what her father had taught her. *Sense the moment.* She slowly let the parchment holding the rest of Tann's speech slip through her fingers, leaving the rest of it unread. She held her hands out to the crowd. "Say it with me: 'Our peace shall be immortal.' "

Rikian stood in the center of the crowd, blinking back tears, as the crowd chanted, "Our peace shall be immortal. Our peace shall be immortal." Mothers cried, holding their infants. Men moved closer to their young sons and daughters, openly wiping tears from their own faces. Rikian leaned toward a large man nearby, and whispered in his ear. "Queen Byrn, the Immortal."

The man looked around, but saw no one. Had the thought been his own? He liked the sound of it, and bellowed out, "Queen Byrn, the Immortal."

Soon the entire crowd chanted it: "Queen Byrn, the Immortal. Queen Byrn, the Immortal."

The leadership tent had been placed near the front of the Guild's encampment outside of Riverbend Fortress. The men sat inside, pensive and without conversation. When news of

Byrn's speech had reached the army, most of the hired soldiers had simply left, without warning and without their pay. The army that remained was still a substantial force, though not one with which attacking a fortress would be advised. And they knew it.

But to leave now would mean their eventual death. Even with the Princess alive in Stonecrop, the King would still see them dead for their treason. They were dead men, one way or the other.

A man ducked into the tent. "Couple of old men here, to talk to you. Not armed."

"Let them in," the man sighed.

The soldiers marched to the front gate of Riverbend Fortress. It was a terrible spot to be in. They felt the deaths of innocent families weighing upon them, whether they had taken part in the raid or not. But they had taken blood oaths to the throne. To abandon such an oath could not be done. They were dead men walking, whether they stayed or left. But they had heard the bugles from the other side of the moat, and so they approached cautiously.

On the other bank, a band of men stood in a line, dingy sheets carried between them. In the center, a banner flew. It was a beautiful banner, lined with ribbons, and carrying the lone symbol of a flower. "We wish to talk," a voice boomed out.

The soldiers stepped forward, their own amplification cone in hand. "Whom do you represent?"

The answer came back clearly. "Her Grace, Byrn, the Duchess of Stonecrop."

The men froze. It had seemed another hopeless shift guarding the Fortress, but now, even simple soldiers such as these knew their lives depended on this answer.

"Should we ask the King?"

The patrol leader looked anxiously up at the Fortress above. *The oath—perhaps there was another way.* "Lower the bridge."

Fisk threw a plate across the room. "Jhol!" How dare she show her face again? He had shown her mercy, and in return she dared challenge him? And to find his own men had gone to attend her imbecilic little speech, without the King's own permission? The cheering crowds would see each of their heads roll for this.

Fisk glared at the thick wooden door. Where was his Captain? How dare he keep the King waiting? Fisk would make him pay as well. In fact, he was due for a changeover of his entire guard, he thought furiously.

"Jhol! Jhol! Don't make me call you again. Get in here!" Where was the insolent man—he had serious work to accomplish and a sister to kill. The door opened, and two older men walked in, grim expressions on their face. Panic gripped Fisk. He knew these men, knew that his guards had been given specific orders never to let either of them near him. Fisk stepped backward, stumbling over his own feet, and grasping wildly at his desk to keep from falling further. "You! How dare they let you in? Where is Jhol? If you have harmed him I will slash your—"

"Shut your mouth, child. Jhol has not been harmed; he and his men are simply no longer interested in your protection." The Duke walked slowly toward him, lowering his voice to a raspy whisper. "You killed her, didn't you? My Marta?"

"Your whore? What of it? She grew troublesome."

The Duke smiled, pride in his eyes. "She fought you, didn't she? Probably almost won." The Duke kicked the unsuspecting King to the floor and then stepped on Fisk's chest, holding him down firmly.

Behind him approached the former Steward of Stonecrop, King Korta's long-time friend and confidant, actually a senior member of the spy network run by the percher elves. The Steward spoke with a chilling confidence. "You ought to know: my name is Issac Dwarve, and I am—and have always been—a spy. I work for your sister now." Issac glanced behind him at the Duke. "Anything else you want to say to him?" The Duke closed his eyes and shook his head.

"Then may your trespasses be forgiven, as you forgive those who trespass against you." Issac reached forward, and before the King even understood what was about to happen, the old spy snapped Fisk's neck. The two men stepped back, as the former King of Fayen lay dead upon the floor of the room where his father had also died, though peacefully, before him and before his sister, only two seasons before.

Byrn walked slowly to the dais, understanding that this ceremony, as all royal ceremony, was more for the subjects—for their closure—than for her own glory. But she must go through with it, exuding brilliance every second, as Tann had coached her, and as her own mother had done artfully for many years.

The Holy Father, leader of the Church, stood before her. "The Creator blesses you, Byrn, daughter of Korta. You are Chosen to rule the land of Fayen." He reached forward, his hand shaking. He held a ring made of a brilliant red metal, with a simple shape of a flower engraved in its center. It was set with no gemstones, yet it sparkled in the light as if it were made of the sunset itself. It was the embodiment of simplicity, and yet it was the most beautiful thing she had ever seen.

She slipped the ring on, and it felt heavy on her finger. *I will never forget the weight that I carry,* she swore silently to herself.

As she walked down the steps outside the Cathedral, she bowed deeply to the three men—or elves, as only she knew them to be—standing at the base of the stairs. "I am forever in your debt."

"It was our pleasure," Rikian responded. Tann nodded, tears in his eyes. Jeekra gave a small, but elegant, bow. Byrn closed her eyelids then opened them. Jeekra smiled, for he knew that she could not let the subjects see her bow to anyone. Not so soon. But the gesture was there all the same. *She will be a fine Queen,* Jeekra mused.

That night, the three elves indulged in a large bottle of royal mead as they sailed away, down the Royal River, on a boat that Tann had rented. The waves lapped gently against the sides as the boat swayed in a pleasant rocking motion.

"When we reach Riverbend, I might not follow you back to the village," Tann tested the waters with this statement.

Jeekra looked up curiously. "Where will we tell the Eldest you have gone?"

"I've not been to most of the northern lands. Not just the human city of Tharta, but also the wolflands, or the coastal islands to the east. They say it is lovely country."

Jeekra nodded appreciatively. "I have been that way. The islands are worth seeing. I will reassure the Eldest it is time well-spent." Jeekra smiled.

Tann noticed that Rikian remained silent. "Rikian?"

"Oh, I agree that you should. Sometimes I wish I spent more time out and about." Rikian gazed wistfully at the clouds.

"You could come with me, Rikian. I am sure I would enjoy the company."

Rikian smiled. He knew Tann well enough to appreciate that the elf preferred being left alone. It was a kind offer.

"I wish I could, friend Tann. But my friends—" Rikian's eyes softened.

Tann nodded. The magnolia elf tended the gardens at the elven village, and Rikian's closeness to the plants that grew there was well-known. It was touching. But Tann's creatures were small birds, short-lived and migratory by nature. He had no such ties.

"It was the girl's idea, actually," Tann offered. "She suggested I spend more time exploring Fayen and learning its ways, if I am meant to protect her creatures."

Jeekra smirked. "A gold piece it was Klev who told her to suggest it."

"Stinking Dwarves," Tann glowered. "You're probably right. But . . . I suppose there are worse faults than to be swayed by a pleasant smile." Tann leaned back into his seat. "I am not one for human looks, but she is a beautiful girl."

"She is," Jeekra agreed.

Rikian said nothing, but smiled and took a sip of mead.

The door creaked behind her and Byrn turned sharply, whisking a small knife into her hand. If her security had let someone in without a summons, it had better be important. Fortunately, the Dwarves had taught her self-defense, enough to give her a chance.

It was a man, alone. An assassin? A rival? A friend? Her heart pounded against her chest. She positioned her knife carefully, though it was still hidden under her flowing lace sleeves.

Dot rushed from the washroom, a broom in her hand. Byrn turned to face the visitor, and gasped. "No, Dot! It's ok. Thank you, but this is an ally, and a pleasant surprise. Please, friend, leave us." Dot scowled, but walked slowly out of the room, still gripping the broom handle tightly. When the door shut, Byrn set her knife down, and smiled. "You're not a man. I see it in your eyes. But, really, doesn't your kind ever knock?"

"My Lady, I am sorry to have startled you. My village, it does not have doors as you would envision them, so we often forget your customs. I am not used to human ways, but in time I am certain that I will learn them."

"In time? Then you are here to stay?"

"Only if you will have me, and keep my true nature a secret. I was sent to assist with whatever it is you might need. At least for a while, to help maintain the peace."

"That would be an honor." She extended her hand. "I am Queen Byrn of Stonecrop."

The elf took her hand, and then bowed deeply. "Within these walls, I shall be known simply as Stinli. And you, I suspect you will be known by the name the people now call you: Byrn the Immortal, of the castle city of Byrntown, ruler of all Fayen."

A tear formed in Byrn's eyes, and she looked away. "Dot, please come back. And leave the broom. There is someone I'd like you to meet."

The End

Three hundred years later, terror has enveloped the land of Fayen. The youngest elven protector, deranged and secluded, twists her blessing to enslave creatures rather than to serve them. And no new elves have been placed in centuries, leaving the others to wonder if their end—or even an end to all things—is drawing near.

In the elven village, the few protectors who remain go about their business, while silently convinced that all is lost. But one elf, Tann Skycaller, has a secret. A secret that may be the salvation of Fayen, restoring liberty to the creatures he was sworn to protect.

Read about this epic journey in the fantasy novel *Spireseeker*, available in paperback and e-book formats from all major retailers, and also in signed hardcover at http://spireseeker.com.